THE VELVET KEY SERIES
AMELIA
The Hotel

DD LORENZO

THE HOTEL: AMELIA

Copyright ©2025 DD Lorenzo

All Rights Reserved.

The Hotel: Amelia is a work of fiction, Names, characters, businesses, organizations, places, events, and incidents either are the product of the author's imagination or are used fictitiously. Any resemblance to actual persons, living or dead, events, or locales is entirely coincidental.

Cover designed by Samantha Cole

Alpha reading by Nicki Webber

Editing by Alyssa Nazzaro, Hundred Proof Service

Proofreading by Michelle Fewer

No part of this book may be reproduced, scanned or distributed in any printed or electronic form without permission. Please do not participate in or encourage piracy of copyrighted materials in violation of the author's rights. Purchase only authorized editions.

For my mother.

When I was young, and read my stories to you, you said that someday my words would matter and they would find their way to the hearts and minds of many readers. Each one bears a quiet mark of you as you lovingly and patiently listened to me spin my tales onto a typewritten page. With every book I craft, I become more of what we always believed was my destiny...

To be a storyteller.

Introduction

There are places that exist beyond the realm of possibility, some of which have stood since time began. Their names have changed throughout the centuries, whispered in legend, buried in forgotten tongues. And yet, the story of their origin remains the same.

This is the story of The Haven.

It was the first.

The root.

The breath before the name.

Born of a need the world did not yet understand, The Haven was created to hold what could not be seen, to heal what could not be spoken. It is from this sanctuary that all other Haven sanctuaries were born. None are shaped by stone or hand, but by longing.

These Havens do not appear on maps. Their addresses do not exist. Their doors do not open for all. They open for The Chosen.

I know all this for I am Elias.

I have watched them.

For as long as time has been, and before the first soul had shone its light, I have existed. Before the first whisper turned to silence, I watched as humankind stepped into existence, brilliant, unbroken, and blind to what they carried within. Born whole yet always striving. Gifted, yet doubtful.

In searching, they forgot themselves.

The world does not nurture the truths they are given at birth. It erodes them. It drowns them in duty and noise, reshaping them into something smaller, something manageable, until they can no longer hear the voice inside themselves. The one that remembers.

Not all are chosen.

But those who are, those whose souls are ripe for reckoning, are called with an invitation.

When they arrive, they find not The Haven itself, but the place their soul believes will soothe them.

A quiet stretch of sea.

A forgotten forest path.

A mirror hidden in the shape of desire.

The dwelling appears as what they need most.

But the journey... ah, the journey... is always deeper.

Each Chosen receives a single key, but the first was carved from the remains of a lightning-struck Ashwood tree, its shape born of destruction, and its surface smoothed by hand over and over until the wood felt like velvet against the skin. Juliette was the first to receive one, and it opened The Haven to her.

Those who follow her receive their own, and when the time comes, when the soul is ready to remember, the calling arrives. Not in the way one expects but in the way one best receives.

An escape.

A whisper in a dream.

An invitation forgotten, then suddenly found.

A slip of gold-edged parchment that was never placed yet has always been.

What follows is left to their fate.

I do not interfere. I watch.

Their struggles. Their choices. The paths they carve for themselves…

Each Chosen has an opportunity to reveal what was buried beneath the forgetting.

Some will break. Some will rise. All will be tested.

To the world, these places are invisible, but to the weary, they are a sanctuary, and to the broken, an unspoken vow.

Once inside, they are something more.

A seduction.

A challenge.

A reckoning.

Forces are at work all around us. Entities of purpose who exist beyond the Veil. Some will raise doubt.

Others will offer peace. They are not seen but heard within and deeply felt. They stretch the imagination to see beyond what is possible, shifting and moving in silent conversation. They tempt those who resist change, luring them with the impossible and daring them to surrender.

But the dwellings—they are more patient. Only those willing to be stripped bare of illusion are welcomed.

They do not seduce.

They wait.

Their walls listen.

Their air hums with the forbidden yet familiar in an ache too deep to name.

They are not entirely magic.

They are alive.

They challenge, observe, and hunger.

They test what lies within the soul.

Some Chosen linger within for moments that feel stretched into eternity, while others leave before night's last hush and carry the weight of their experience for a lifetime. Yet, no matter where or when they arrive, every soul crosses the threshold the same.

Welcome.

Your velvet key awaits.

History

Juliette Elisabeth Armand was born into a world gilded with expectation. The year was 1752, and the name she carried, Armand, was heavy with legacy. Influence, refinement, and silent obligation laced every corridor of her upbringing. As the only daughter of a powerful lineage, she was cradled in privilege but raised on precision. From the moment her small feet touched polished floors, her mother taught her the quiet choreography expected of women like them, the art of existing without error, of pleasing without passion, of becoming what others needed before ever knowing who she was.

Her mother, a woman of unyielding precision, governed Juliette's upbringing with an iron hand.

She did not see her daughter as an individual but as an investment that must be polished, molded, and prepared for transaction. She often reminded Juliette that a woman's most significant currency was her ability to conform. Anything else, emotion, individuality, longing, was a flaw to be corrected.

But Juliette was not easily molded.

She felt things too deeply: the unspoken tension in a room, the sadness behind polite smiles, the way the world pulsed with emotions too heavy for those around her to carry. She learned to quiet herself and play the role expected of her, but beneath her graceful demeanor burned an ember of defiance that refused to die.

When suitors came, carefully chosen for their wealth and title, Juliette met their advances with wit and charm, deflecting them like a seasoned diplomat. She did not rebel openly. But she resisted in the only ways she could.

Her father, by contrast, moved through the world like a hush. He seldom interrupted the symphony of his wife's instruction, choosing instead the shadows of silence over the sharp edge of interference. Yet, Juliette felt his gaze, a quiet presence that bore witness to the weight she carried. He saw her, truly saw her, in the rare moments between lessons and rehearsals, when the mask slipped and the ache for freedom showed in her eyes. He never named it, but she knew he recognized it. And though his mouth rarely formed the words, she sensed the guilt that lived inside him, a quiet sorrow for loving a woman who clipped their daughter's wings, and for standing still while it happened.

Then came the disaster.

The Armand fortune, once a source of power and security, began to unravel. Insurmountable debts birthed rumors of ruin. What was once unthinkable became unavoidable. Her mother, desperate, sought to leverage Juliette in a final act of preservation, a marriage that would ensure survival, a transaction dressed as a proposal.

Her father, bound by duty but driven by love, made a different choice.

As Juliette's birthday approached, he called her to his study, an act so rare she knew it was of great importance. He said little. Instead, he placed a purse of coins into her hands, his fingers curling over hers for the briefest moment. It was an unspoken act of love, penance, a gift, and an apology. His voice, thick with emotion, uttered a single word.

"Go."

Juliette understood everything in that moment.

She did not wait.

That night, beneath the cover of darkness, she left behind the world that had been laid out for her and stepped into the unknown.

She traveled across Europe, following the whisper of adventure wherever it led. She danced in the golden light of Venetian masquerades. She traced the ruins of lost civilizations with her fingertips. She stood on windswept cliffs where the sky met the sea. She drank in the stories of strangers, learning that every face carried a history, every heart a longing.

Yet no matter how far she wandered, she could not escape the quiet war within her, the tension between her need for belonging and her refusal to conform.

She had left her mother's world behind. But its ghost still clung to her.

With time, the purse of coins, once a symbol of freedom, grew lighter. As the last of Juliette's resources dwindled, so did her illusions of boundless escape.

Perhaps her mother had been right.

A woman must do what she must to survive.

With reluctant acceptance, she boarded a ship bound for home, bracing herself for the life she had once run from.

But fate had other plans.

A swift and merciless storm descended upon the sea, tearing through the ship with the ferocity of an unspoken truth. With screams swallowed by the wind, the boat splintered. Shattered pieces of wood, mounds of cargo, and Juliette were cast into the abyss.

When she awoke, it was to the scent of earth, damp, ancient, untouched by time, and the wreckage of her former life was behind her. She had been carried, not by luck, but by something greater, delivered to the threshold of a place that existed outside of anything she had ever known.

A sanctuary veiled in mist.

A realm where the air thrummed with something both ancient and alive.

The Haven.

For the first time in her life, there were no expectations, watchful eyes, or demands that she be anything but what she was. The walls whispered, but not of duty—they whispered of possibility.

And when the last of her illusions fell away, he appeared.

Elias.

More myth than man, he did not come with answers. He did not offer salvation. Instead, he asked questions.

Why do you seek approval from a world that does not see you?

Why do you fear the silence of standing still?

Who are you when stripped of all that has been placed upon you?

Within The Haven, Juliette unraveled the years of conditioning, shedding the weight of expectation thread by thread.

She did not become something new.

She simply became herself.

And in that quiet becoming, Elias saw something in her.

The Haven existed long before Juliette arrived. It had whispered across centuries, beckoning lost souls toward transformation. But something had been missing, something more.

A prophecy that had not yet been fulfilled: The Call of The Seeker.

Juliette was the answer. She was the first Chosen.

A place needed to exist beyond The Haven's walls, a vessel for seekers, where transformation was not given, but chosen.

And so, Juliette did what she was always meant to do.

She became the steward and the architect of invitation.

She created a way that one's place of respite would meet their desires and their needs.

Now, across time and reality, The Haven bridges a gap. Venues appear made up of a Chosen's dreams and longings. It becomes visible to those ready to embrace it but remains hidden to humankind who resist change.

And in the wake of their shadows, Juliette remains.

She is not bound by time nor forgotten by history.

She is a presence ever-felt and ever-watching.

For those who enter a Haven creation, she can be both mystery and guide.

For those who listen, she is a comforting whisper in the dark.

For those who dare answer, she is the key that assists in unlocking the soul.

I

"You never know what fate has in store, Amelia."

I throw a glare at my assistant, Sophie. "I don't believe in fate—though, I'm sure it can be a comforting illusion." I won't be the one to burst Sophie's pretty pink bubble, but I think fate is an excuse those who are weak tell themselves when they lack the will to seize control. I'm sure there are many who surrender responsibility to the ever-shifting tides of life.

I'm not like them.

I don't surrender. I thrive on control. It courses through my veins, electric and absolute. It's always been the steady pulse beneath every decision I make. Control built Daniels Enterprises into the empire it is today, and I've spent years wielding and sculpting its future with relentless focus and unwavering intent.

At least, I used to.

Back then, every move I made was calculated, and every risk weighed. I sacrificed sleep, relationships, and pieces of myself for success. I've been described as a woman with sharp blue eyes and a matching resolve that can cut through steel. I shattered ceilings, outmaneuvered competitors, and never once second-guessed my choices.

I don't believe in destiny.

I believe in power.

And now, the whispers have begun.

"She has no soul." "She cares more about success than she does about people." "Does she even feel anything?"

The accusers murmur in the corridors when they think I cannot hear. Except now, they're no longer whispers in the corridors. My staff has gone to the Board of Directors.

MY staff.

Sophie is the only one I trust anymore. The others tell them I am impossible to work with. That I'm too demanding. Too controlling. And they are not going to stand for it any longer.

I lean over my desk, pressing my palms flat against the cold surface, trying to force the anger down, to bury it beneath reason, but it refuses to go quietly. I've built all of this with my own wit and intelligence. And now they want to rip it from me because I'm too much? Too much what?

Too strong?

Too demanding?

Too unwilling to bend for the comfort of those who will never know the price of building something from nothing.

Screw them.

They don't know what I've gone through to become the person I am.

I straighten, stiffening my spine as I inhale sharply. Fine. If my employees think I need to change, I'll take a vacation and examine my approach. I thought my company was comprised of professionals but they're whining like little babies. I'll reset to keep the peace, and when I get back, I'll show them what change looks like. I'll go somewhere new. Somewhere fresh.

Little do they know I've been thinking of taking a vacation since last week, though I would never admit it aloud. Even as I bury myself in schedules and board reports, there's been a tension simmering beneath the surface—a restlessness I can't quite name. The kind that clings to you at night, pressing behind your eyes when the world goes quiet. If Sophie wants me to believe in fate, I'll play along. The universe—if there is such a thing in the way she describes—must have been listening to my thoughts when I discovered The Hotel.

The first nudge came late one night, while fighting another losing battle with insomnia. Sleep has long been an indulgence. My mind is endlessly restless, my thoughts too sharp to surrender to dreams. Instead, I lie awake, scrolling mindlessly through my phone, allowing the cold glow of the screen to fill the silence.

And that's when it appeared.

A single post.

An image of a grand, ivy-draped building, its windows spilling golden light like a secret. Beneath it is a caption.

The place where I found myself.

#TheHotel

Something hitched in my chest. One word snagged my thoughts as my thumb hovered over the image.

Transformation?

The thought is absurd. I have spent my entire life shaping myself into the woman I am. I don't need to be transformed, and yet, something about the word tugs at me with an almost undeniable pull.

I tapped on the profile, curiosity slipping through the cracks of logic—and then, in the pause before I blinked, it vanished. The post. The account. Everything. I refreshed the feed. Nothing. Searched hashtags. Nothing. Not even a trace in my browser history. It was as if it had never existed at all. My rational mind scrambled for explanations—a glitch, a dream, an exhausted hallucination—but something deeper stirred. A whisper that maybe it hadn't been an error. Maybe it had been... intentional.

I rolled over, swiping my thumb up and down the screen, thinking maybe it was the algorithm. Doubt curled around my ribs, tightening like a whispered secret. I was exhausted and thought maybe my muddled brain mixed up a few posts and I didn't see what I thought I saw.

I shifted to my side and set my phone down on the bedside table, then flipped to my back. Inhaling slowly, I pulled in a lungful of air. I closed my eyes and felt myself slipping into unconsciousness, but before sleep finally claimed me, thoughts of The Hotel lingered in the back of my mind.

By dawn, I nearly forgot.

Nearly.

The next morning, I arrived at the office ready for a day's work and grateful to be busy. There's always another meeting, crisis, or flood of emails demanding my attention, so I dive in. While I'm sitting at my desk reviewing, Sophie steps into the office and sets some mail on my desk.

"This looks fancy," she teases in a singsong voice.

I can't help but muster a smile. Sophie's been with me for years and gauges my mercurial moods well.

She knows when to be silent and when to be playful. This morning is a mix of both because she's well aware of the tension between me and the staff. I arch a brow, amused as I take in an elegant black envelope resting atop the stack of work. The paper is thick and weighty between my fingertips.

I slide my letter opener beneath the seam and, like a coaxed secret, the sealed edge parts. I reach inside and pull out an equally luxurious card made of solid black, heavyweight paper embossed with a golden key. Beneath it, written in elegant script, are the words:

Disappear. Escape. Discover.
The Hotel.

My fingers drift along the raised design, tracing its edges like a secret waiting to speak. Something loosens beneath my ribs as I unfold the brochure. The images don't simply appear; they flicker, like memories just out of reach. They feature a pond shimmering beneath a wash of moonlight, its surface kissed by the reflection of stars and surrounded by blooms that seem to hum with quiet invitation. Next, an endless hall of mirrors stretches into mystery, reflecting not what is, but what could be. The final photo showcases a sun-drenched suite, too beautiful to be real, as if the room itself is waiting in stillness. The Hotel hums on the page with unmitigated luxury, alive in a way I can't explain, as though it knows I'm watching. Like a secret aching to be remembered, the words are few, and don't need to shout...

A sanctuary for those adrift.
A key to your forgotten self.
Your journey awaits.

And somehow, I know those words were written for me.

I press my palm against the rich matte paper as a strange feeling twists low in my stomach. No one but me knows how I searched for this during the night, and it seems like such a coincidence. Why am I seeing this again? And a hotel called "The Hotel"? I've been all over the world yet have never heard of this place. It's almost like it's reading my mind.

Scoffing at the ridiculous thought, I remind myself I don't believe in fate, and I don't believe in signs. Yet, as I sit here with The Hotel's invitation, I can't shake the feeling that I'm seeing this now for a reason.

Sophie leans over my shoulder. "Not that I'm trying to influence you, Amelia, but maybe you should treat yourself. This place looks amazing."

"Stop being nosey," I chuckle.

"I'm just saying..." She shrugs playfully, smiling as she comes around to the front of my desk.

A clicking sound fills the room as I repeatedly tap the brochure against the surface. Sophie watches, then gives me a concerned look.

"There's a lot going on here, Boss. I can feel something boiling beneath the surface. Tensions have been high; you know it, and I know it. Would it be such a bad idea for you to take some time to clear your head? You haven't taken a vacation in years, Amelia. Go away for a week. All of this will still be here when you get back."

A pucker pulls my lips aside, and I stare at my assistant, whose loyalty is without question. She's more than an assistant—more than staff. She's the one person who's stayed, who's endured every storm I've brought to this office and answered it with grace. Her concern stirs something I don't let myself feel often: the ache of being seen. Not as a boss. Not as a machine. Just... as a woman trying to hold it all together.

"I'll think about it, Soph," I murmur, the brochure still warm beneath my fingertips. "Promise."

2

Two days later, the blade in my back feels cold enough to burn me. I stare aimlessly out at the apex of my world. The vibrant springtime vision outside my office window stretches on while I sit encased in glass and steel. I knew my employees were unhappy, but the truth of an uprising slapped me this morning and unsettles and unravels me in ways I can barely comprehend.

Six months ago, I was featured in Forbes magazine, the cover now matted and beautifully framed on my wall.

> *Building Power: How Amelia Daniels Built One of the Most Influential Women-Owned Construction Firms in the U.S.*

When I stormed into my office, I snatched The Hotel's marketing materials off my desk in an angry huff. All I want to do is get away from this place, and as I run my thumb back and forth over the feel of the raised, embossed key, I find no solace in its golden sheen. I have to get away to clear my head. Away from all of them—from all of this—and I get the feeling The Hotel could be the sanctuary I need.

Plopping into my chair, I nudge the rollerball and activate the desktop. A few minutes later, I'm dismayed to learn there is little to find on The Hotel, and what I do see on social media seems to disappear almost as quickly as I uncover it. Is it that damned exclusive that the public isn't welcome?

No sooner do I think the thought than the website appears like magic. It wasn't there a moment ago. Not in the search results. Not in any open tabs. But now, suddenly, it's here—as if waiting for me to want it badly enough.

My fingers hover above the keyboard, the sudden flash of the screen catching me off guard. It's a good thing because without reading some reviews, I'd usually throw a brochure like this in the trash, no matter how pretty it looks. Now that it popped up in the search, the unknown doesn't feel as threatening.

After perusing the images for a few minutes, I decide that it does appear The Hotel is an exclusive, invitation-only type resort. Usually, that kind of secrecy would make me shut it down. But there's something about this that feels different—not dangerous. Just... deliberate.

I've never been to one, but it seems like a great place. The reviews rave about customer experiences.

I think on it for a minute, warring with myself. My current situation at work is crappy, and if I lean into Sophie's mindset, the universe has intervened and provided me with a perfect opportunity for escape exactly at a time I need it—but I don't want it to seem like I'm running away. The Hotel is a new place to discover, which intrigues me. And I do need a vacation...

The Board—those bastards—gave me an ultimatum: change my attitude or...

Or what?

Wildfire rages through my blood and penetrates emotions I've built walls around. Feelings of betrayal rise inside me once again. I sat in that boardroom with my fist-clenched hands hidden in my lap. It was torture. Especially when I heard the words, "Amelia, the employees are threatening to walk. All of them. You're out of control…"

I wanted to fire back, "Let them walk! This is my damn company!" Instead, I kept my mouth shut.

They owe their careers to the business I built. And now I'm the villain? Sitting there felt like being sent to the principal's office. How do they think you get the most out of people? You push, not mollycoddle them. Do they believe corporations are built on kindness? That companies like mine are simply handed to women? They're out of their minds if they think I'll go quietly. I've bled most of my adult life away for this place. I sacrificed for its growth and to perfect its business practices. According to them, I'm too hard on everybody, too driven, and I expect the impossible: perfection. Ha! They wouldn't know perfection if it bit them on the ass.

I exhale a resigned sigh. The final "recommendation" came from a consensus of the Board: "A little vacation would do you good, Amelia. You know… to change your outlook."

What the bastards really want is for me to become something lesser than what I am.

If I were a man, they would sing a different tune; they know it, and I know it.

They'd say I was ballsy.

That I'm a shrewd businessperson.

Because I'm a woman, they want something softer. Weaker.

Their ultimatum echoes in my head like a venomous hiss, and I'm not sure I'll ever forgive them.

The glass walls in this room showcase the city skyline. I conquered it, and I need to remind all of them of the facts and how rare women-owned construction companies like mine are. But how?

High above the city, the endless hum of life merges with tree dots in the steel-towered landscape I've created through my company. I should feel victorious, and typically, I do. Today, they've stripped it from me, leaving only the hollow ache of what I've built. I'm robbed of that golden glory called success and feel I'm a queen on the throne of a kingdom that no longer belongs to me. It was a calculated boardroom coup, and the fact that John, my most trusted ally, held the blade that stabbed me pierced something deeper than my flesh. He once toasted me with champagne and called me unstoppable. Now, he's just another knife in the dark.

His betrayal sinks into the garnet abyss of my heart—the very one he accuses me of not having.

I close my eyes, shaking my head in disbelief.

If I wasn't so tough, I would cry.

Maybe I am an ice queen.

A scream escapes disguised as a sigh. All my efforts seem moot at the moment. When I think of the endless sleepless nights, the ruined relationships, and the personal life I traded for contracts...

The people I trusted weaponized my hard-ass ways against me. They've twisted my work ethic, painted me as a ruthless, disconnected, and unfeeling bitch, and made me feel like I outlived my purpose.

Assholes.

To hell with them.

The sun shifts, casting my reflection on the glass. A poised woman stares back at me, sharp in her suit, electric blue eyes unyielding. I see the fault line spidering beneath the flawless makeup, a crack no one else would dare notice.

And it scares the hell out of me.

A chime signals an incoming email, interrupting my thoughts. I'm grateful for the distraction and return to my desk. The beautiful, custom, high-back executive chair that cradles me daily now feels more like a cage. My palm meets the curve of the mouse, a motion half-forgotten by muscle memory and half-anchored in precision. A couple of emails rush in as the screen lights, but it's one subject line that captures my attention.

Unlock the Door to Your Future.

I hesitate, my cursor hovering over the email before I click to open it, and then I do.

There is no greater luxury than clarity. The Hotel awaits.

My stomach tightens. My gaze flicks to the time in the corner of my screen.

4:44

Sophie constantly notes that number and sends me screenshots of when it appears on her phone or when she sees it while she's out. She says it's a number of guidance and alignment. At the moment, it feels like a number that's less like a coincidence and more like a whisper.

An uncustomary stillness creeps in. Somehow, the air in my office feels thicker, like walking through a humid August day. All of a sudden it turns suffocating and I struggle to pull in air. The invitation to The Hotel is still on my screen. I respond by clicking the link for availability, and a sleek form appears, classic in its elegance. It asks one question.

When will your journey begin?

I hover the cursor over tomorrow's date, then click to submit. The response is instantaneous.

Welcome. Your velvet key awaits.

As I stare at the screen, my eyes are momentarily glued to it. Am I really doing this?

A knock at my door pulls me to the present. Sophie timidly steps inside, her expression grim.

"They asked me to check your calendar. They want to see you again—tomorrow."

"I can't." Defiantly, I raise my chin and stiffen my spine until I pull myself to my full height.

A wary Sophie watches me. "Can I give them a reason?"

I blink away the sting of tears as I grab my bag and tuck it beneath my arm. I'm not sure if I'm more angry than hurt because that part of my emotional well went dry a long time ago—when I was taught to ignore my feelings.

"Tell them whatever you want. I'm out of here for a week."

"Good afternoon, Ms. Daniels. I'm your transport to The Hotel."

I offer a nod to the driver as he opens the door to the waiting limousine. Once I'm settled inside, he places my luggage into the trunk, then quietly slips behind the wheel. The door closes with a soft thud, and just like that, we're moving. No small talk. No welcome packet or itinerary, unlike in my previous meetings. Just golden, blissful silence.

The farther we drive from the city, the more my chest loosens. The tension I carried from the office yesterday has settled deep into my bones with a heaviness that made sleep nearly impossible. I hadn't realized how tightly wound I was until this silence began to stretch around me. My shoulders ache in unfamiliar places as they drift to a more natural position. My jaw unclenches. It seems my body is just now discovering how long it's been braced for impact and is coming to rest, and as more of the skyline blurs behind us, more of me unclenches.

I take one last glance as the company I thought I commanded shrinks away. The glass towers and concrete crowns surrounding my domain recede into the distance, giving way to space and stillness. I pour myself a glass of wine from the chilled bottle waiting beside me, grateful for the quiet as the world I've built fades into irrelevance—if only for now.

The hum of the drive continues to lull me as I glance down at the only tangible evidence I have that The Hotel exists; the invitation resting in my lap. I still don't understand how or why it found me. No matter how much Sophie tries to convince me, I can't wrap my head around divine timing or cosmic connection. Coincidence is just a pattern misread. A convenient story we tell ourselves to make sense of the random. And yet... there's something about this place—about The Hotel—that unsettles me. That pulls at me and feels, impossibly, like recognition. Maybe Sophie's right.

I push the thought aside and finish my wine. Just as the last of it warms my throat, the car slows down. The two glasses of cabernet provided for me suffice to relax me, and I secure the glass, now looking at this experience with less of an edge. When I glance out the window, my body locks.

The majesty catches me instantly as iron gates rise into view, tall, dark, and formidable. Their intricate black metalwork twists into the shape of a golden key at the center, gleaming against the wrought iron like a secret locked in plain sight. No sign. No nameplate. No luxury branding. Only the gold key —just like the invitation.

The gates melt into a mist that curls at the edges of connecting ivy-draped stone walls. Endlessly, they stretch until I can no longer see them within the fog, as if the world beyond is deliberately hidden.

As the driver steps out and opens my door, I tuck the invitation away, and it somehow feels heavier. It's as if it's gathered weight during the silent ride, absorbing an energetic burden. Perhaps I released tension, and it soaked it in. But that's impossible.

The absurd thought makes me smile and makes me think of the one person back at the office who I still have in my corner.

As I step out of the car, a jittery feeling sneaks in. I've walked into million-dollar boardrooms and signed contracts that altered skylines, never with a flicker of doubt. And yet, standing at this threshold, I feel exposed.

"Ms. Daniels," the driver catches my attention with a low, warm voice. "Please check your phone and enter the numbers you see into the gate box."

As if on cue, my phone buzzes. A message flashes on the screen.

The Hotel
M131J

Beneath the code, there's an image of a key box, an exact replica of the one embedded in the gate. I step forward and type it in.

In an instant, a low hum stirs the air. The gates don't just part; they yield, opening slowly, almost reverently, as they recognize the letters and numbers.

"My bag?" I ask, needing something familiar to ground me.

"It will be taken to your suite, ma'am," the driver replies, his voice smooth and practiced.

"No," I quickly reply. "I'll take it myself."

He meets my gaze, calm and unbothered. "I assure you; it will be safe. Your time at The Hotel is meant to be one of ease."

My brow crunches as I offer a weak nod. I hesitate. Business trips have been my only travel in years, and I rarely let my bag out of my sight. Handing it over seems like a small act, but it lands somewhere deeper, as if I'm loosening a thread inside me that's been kept tight.

Out of nowhere, a pang of guilt hits me, and I hesitate to move forward. Why am I here? I should be back in the office, fighting to keep what's mine. I should be holding meetings, demanding accountability, reestablishing order and my authority. Instead, I'm standing at the gates of some opulent mystery, waiting for something I can't even name.

Clarity?

Escape?

Reckoning?

Maybe all three. I haven't had much time to think

about it and make a decision. "Oh, what the hell. I'm here already…"

A slight shiver moves through me as I step forward. The shift in atmosphere is subtle, but it's there. It feels like I'm walking into a dream I haven't yet remembered, and when I see the courtyard, I stand amazed. It. Is. Extraordinary.

Massive old-growth trees arch toward the sky, their ancient limbs forming a canopy that scatters light like falling gold. The ground beneath my feet glitters, a mosaic path made of glass studded with keys of every shape and size. Each key is etched with a single word. I catch glimpses as I walk.

Forgive. Remember. Release.

Words that feel less like labels and more like instructions.

Sunny rays dance across the stones as if deliberately spotlighting one key after another. It feels alive. Intentional.

My heels strike the path with quiet purpose, but each step that hits a worded key feels like something else, like I'm stepping into stories that are already written. I glance down at them beneath the glass, each word catching light in turn, and wonder if they're meant to guide me or warn me. Either way, the thick air insists that I walk more slowly and observe. I'm about to round a curve when I look up and see it.

The Hotel.

It rises before me, majestic, timeless, and strange. The architecture shifts between eras, making it impossible to pin down a specific style. Concrete merges with glass, softened by the same ivy that framed the gates. As I draw closer, I notice the plant trail is threaded with color—deep violet veins running through lush green leaves—and the contrast is unsettlingly beautiful.

The tall windows mirror the trees but reveal slivers of warm, sunshiny light inside. The exterior glints with gold, just enough to suggest opulence but not enough to boast. The structure is a paradox: welcoming and guarded, opulent and austere.

A warm feeling comes over me, and for a moment, I feel like it has anticipated my arrival. I barely have time to register the thought when the doors open on their own.

I walk inside, but there's no one in sight. My steps falter. The silence within isn't just absence; it's presence. It's thick and hums through me like low-voltage electricity, and it feels like someone, or something, is watching and waiting.

A flash of white linen catches the corner of my vision, and a man steps forward, tall, handsome, and calm. His movements are fluid and assured. He's dressed in a gossamer shirt and pants, crisp and elegant and unaffected by style or time. His presence is magnetic, but it's his eyes that stop me—deep, deep blue, like an ancient midnight sky and something older than memory.

"Amelia Daniels." I extend my hand, slipping back into my armored CEO shell with practiced ease.

He takes my hand—warm, grounded. "Welcome to The Hotel, Ms. Daniels. I'm Ethan. I'll be your guide during your journey."

"Journey?" The word tastes unfamiliar on my tongue, like something meant for someone else.

He nods, his voice gentle. "The Hotel isn't just a place to stay. It's a passage. A transformation. Some Chosen need a guide as they move through it."

I pause, studying him, caught between skepticism and something I can't quite name. "You keep using that word—Chosen, like this wasn't chance. Like I didn't find you... you found me."

My voice softens. "It didn't feel like a vacation offer. It felt... personal. Like someone knew I was fraying and extended their hand before I realized I needed it."

He doesn't flinch. "Courted is a good word," he says. A flicker of something thoughtful shifts behind his eyes. "The Hotel chose you. It finds those who need its presence. My role is simply to assist you while you're here."

There's no push. No pressure. Just a simple offering.

Still cautious, the word "assist" bristles something inside. I'm not someone who needs help.

He reaches into his pocket and offers a small black velvet box tied with a cream ribbon. The golden key emblem on top matches the one from my invitation, and I can't help but note that The Hotel branding is impeccable.

I hesitate. Logic tells me to be cautious. But something else—something quieter and older—urges me forward.

Curiosity wins.

Inside, resting against folds of dark velvet, is a sleek metal key, its shank etched with an elegant design.

I lift it from the box, and its weight surprises me. It isn't just in substance, but its presence. The crafting is heavy and intentional. The moment it touches my hand, an unusual awareness flares inside with a feeling I find hard to comprehend. I feel silly, projecting meaning onto a piece of metal, but the instant it grazes my fingertips, something in me quiets. Not a simple calm, but more a feeling of alignment. Like cogs and teeth engage something inside of me that's long been locked and now clicks into place.

"There are many doors within The Hotel. I will assist, but your key will guide you to the ones meant for you to open." His voice drops in tone and volume as if we're sharing a secret.

My eyes meet his. I'm about to ask more questions, but I hold back.

Ethan looks at his watch and then smiles up at me. "Your room is ready, but first, I'd like you to meet The Hotel's steward."

I slip the key into my pocket, my fingers curling around it like one of Sophie's worry stones, an anchor for my trepidation. "Lead the way."

The words sound like an order and are sharper than I intend. Ethan simply nods, unaffected, and turns down the corridor. I follow behind and, once again, feel the unknown energy.

The low thrumming seems to rise from the walls themselves. Not a sound exactly, more like a pulse after a pause held too long. It feels like the place has been holding that stillness just for me—and now that I've arrived, it exhales.

Like the place is alive.

Behind the Veil
The Watcher

A TREMOR PASSES through the Veil. Amelia Daniels has crossed the threshold.

Elias pauses as The Hotel registers Amelia's presence, for something within him stills whenever a Chosen crosses the threshold of their haven. He does not blink or stir but perceives her as a ripple through the fabric of becoming. Her arrival is not noise, it is resonance. A quiet disruption in the stillness he's kept vigil over for longer than time can remember.

Beyond the edge of ordinary perception, where architecture bends toward memory and intent, he watches her. This woman, wrapped in armor and ache, walks with the steel-spined resolve of someone used to being observed, yet never truly seen. She carries her past like an old leather attaché, neatly packed, tightly latched, deliberately unexamined. She builds walls out of control and precision, yet now enters a structure that moves with her in quiet awareness.

The Hotel knows what she cannot: that she did not come for rest. She came for reckoning.

Its gates did not open because she knocked, but because her moment of alignment had arrived. The instant her fingertips touched the invitation, the air shifted. The Hotel stirred. A hum passed through its bones, pulling from its chambers old memories and shaping new ones. The walls began to adjust before she ever set foot on the grounds, rearranging themselves according to the architecture of her resistance.

Three corridors deep, behind the Veil, a door begins to warm. Its keyplate pulses faintly with anticipation. A chamber untouched for decades stirs to life without command. It does not question why, for The Hotel does not speculate. It prepares. It simply knows when someone has been seen.

The path representing many souls laid itself in glass. The words beneath her feet shifted to an order she would notice. Ivy outside her window drank in her energy, its violet veins darkening to echo the bruises on her heart. Even the windows, half-reflective and half-revealing, awaited the moment they would show her not who she is, but what she has buried… and what she will birth.

Amelia believes she will rest, but The Hotel sees her deeper desire. She came to save something she cannot yet name. What must be saved is not Daniels Enterprises.

It is Amelia Daniels herself.

What she does not yet know is that her poise, her control, her obsessive composure—these things are not obstacles. They are material. Raw ingredients.

Like limestone before it becomes a cathedral. Like fire before it tempers steel. The Hotel does not see her perfection as armor, but as an invitation. A summons to crack, soften, to break. It is necessary for something true to arise.

From behind the Veil, Elias watches.

He does not interfere, but when The Hotel exhales —he listens.

Because it is a beginning.

And Amelia, though unaware, has already begun to change.

4

I follow Ethan to a wooden door, rich in color and polished to a beautiful shine. A brass plaque rests about a quarter of the way down, engraved with elegant, sweeping script:

She Receives. She Guides.

It isn't the words that stop me; it's the door itself. The grain of wood is deeper than others I've seen, its patterns so vivid they seem to move with the light. Subtle golden vines spiral up the lower panels, so delicately etched they seem less carved than coaxed into being, living trails frozen mid-bloom. Among the curling tendrils, tiny emblems emerge, an open lotus cradling a key. The symbols are oddly familiar, like something I've once seen but forgotten.

My gaze drops to the floor. The wood shifts to stone beneath the threshold, and thin lines of gold etching stretch across it. There's an inscription in a language I don't recognize. As I approach, the script glows faintly on its own, and I stop. The hair on my arms lifts. That energy I felt before returns. A soft, almost imperceptible hum resonates through the air, not from the door but from something within it.

Ethan says nothing. He simply places his hand on the sunburst-shaped doorknob and pauses. There's a reverence in the way he touches it, like one might feel the cover of a sacred book.

"This is Esme," he says quietly, the weight of the title hanging in the air.

He smiles as the door glides inward without a sound, revealing a sunlit room lined with soft shelves, hand-carved details, and the subtle scent of lavender and old paper. A desk sits near the tall window, where afternoon light spills across its surface in golden ribbons.

The woman behind the desk rises, poised and expectant. She doesn't rush. There's no performance in her movements, only the calm certainty of someone who's always known how the story ends.

Her hair is the color of cornsilk, shining beneath the afternoon sun, fashioned into an elegant twist. The style suggests effortless control rather than vanity. A simple cobalt-colored suit drapes perfectly over her petite yet tall frame. It's not flashy but exquisitely tailored, with every line precise. She carries her look the way a queen wears a crown, without question or apology.

"Welcome, Ms. Daniels. My name is Esme. I'm the steward of The Hotel. It's a pleasure to meet you." She reaches with an outstretched hand, which I take for an introductory shake as business instincts take over. My grip is firm and measured, a reflex ingrained by years of taking hands over negotiations, mergers, and silent power plays.

"The plaque on the door reads 'She receives. She guides.' What does it mean?"

"It's a simplistic description of my duties. I both welcome guests and guide them on their journey, should they need me. However, 'Esme' is more than a name. All who take it accept both the name and stewardship."

"Interesting." Though my curiosity is piqued, now is not the time for questions, and I have several. I add this one to a mental list that consistently has a place in my mind.

Esme radiates quiet authority, not the kind that demands attention but the kind that exists beyond the need for it. Her tone is calm, smooth, and warm, like the first rays of something familiar, and laced with an appealing and unexpected quality. Her moss-green eyes cast a gaze that feels old yet very much alive. They lock with mine, sharp and knowing.

"Beautiful facility you have here, Esme." My words are smooth, my voice giving no trace of trepidation. I'm well aware of my strengths and weaknesses, and control is my currency. I spend it well. "I'm not familiar with The Hotel. I'm unsure what to expect."

Esme's lips curl into the faintest smile, the kind that suggests she heard my thoughts before they ever reached my mouth. "That's by design, Ms. Daniels," she says, offering nothing more. With a graceful nod, she glides forward, and I fall into step behind her.

The hallway stretches before us like a memory I've never lived but somehow recognize. It isn't garish; no need for that. The elegance here whispers.

Antique sconces line the walls, casting soft, flickering light that dances like echoes. The marble beneath my heels gleams with such perfection it reflects the shimmer above from an elaborate chandelier. Its crystals are shaped like delicate keys and are suspended at various heights and drops. I slow down to soak it in; momentarily caught by the pleasure the sight gives me. There's a quiet rhythm in the way their sway, mesmerizing, deliberate, as if each one waits to open something unnamed, something forgotten. The Hotel doesn't shout its grandeur, yet every detail feels chosen with a caring, measured elegance, tempered beauty, and just enough opulence to make the heart ache. Even the air seems curated. It wears a fragrance that is both haunting and seductive, like a memory trying to return. It lingers at the edge of knowing, velvet-rich, achingly familiar. Yet, it slips away the moment I try to place it. I'm both annoyed and intrigued that it brushes against the edges of memory but never quite settles with focus, almost like a fragrance that teases the mind. At the same time, its name or creator stays just beyond reach.

The farther I walk the hallway with Esme, the more I see that this place doesn't have the synthetic feel of most travel accommodations. It isn't curated—as most chains are—but it seems more enticing than any I've experienced. It presents as a boutique hotel, but something about it pulses with life. It has more of a vibe and feels more alive than any building I've ever stepped inside—both figuratively and literally.

"I'm not sure I've ever seen a more gracious and elegant structure." Suddenly, overwhelmed with how magnificently this building has been created, my thoughts slip out and into words. Even my tone changes in that moment of complete architectural enchantment and bliss. One minute, I sound all business. The next, a quiet softness settles into my voice.

She acknowledges my comment with a nod. "We believe beauty is part of the healing process, but it's only the beginning." She pauses. "May I call you Amelia?"

"Amelia is fine, but—healing?" My forehead pinches. The word strikes something unwelcome inside me; some bruise I didn't know I carried. "Now, I'm confused, Esme. I'm not ill by any means. If that's why I was courted to your facility, a mistake has been made. Perhaps my name appeared on a list somewhere, but in the wrong column. Though I'm a major donor to Make-A-Wish, I'm not one of the people needing help. I assure you, if that's the case, we've both made a mistake."

Esme glances at me as if reading something in my expression—something of which I'm unaware. She pauses, intensifying her focus as she studies me. Then, her expression shifts slightly as a knowing smile gently curls the corners of her mouth. Somehow, I got the feeling when she was looking at me, she wasn't simply looking at my shell but, somehow, was also inside my head.

"There's been no mistake, Amelia. Your intuition led you here."

Intuition.

The word settles inside me, and as I digest it, it sours my stomach. I've spent my life navigating boardrooms. I dictate reality with facts and figures. I'm not into all the 'woo-woo' that Sophie's into, which seems to be the fad. Yet, I accepted the unusual invitation to this place.

"Forgive me, Esme, but intuition is a myth—as are gut feelings, premonitions, and the like."

Esme's movements remain unhurried as I keep pace beside her. She speaks softly, firmly, and passionately. "Unlike you, I know intuition is your guide. It's the divining rod that leads you to what you already know. Some people call it an inner compass or, yes, a gut feeling, but, sadly, most people ignore it until they can barely hear it at all." She stops walking and shifts her gaze to me. "You've ignored it for a very long time, Amelia. But I'm certain your time at The Hotel will satisfy the need to reset."

The implication that I might need anything at all makes the comment press into me like a finger poking into my chest. It's too familiar and too close, causing a discomforting feeling I don't like. I slide my focus in another direction, noting the rows of closed doors we've passed. Each is polished wood adorned with a brass plate, just like Esme's office door, but all are engraved with different symbols. I can't push aside my curiosity, assuming they offer standard hotel amenities I'd like to use, such as a spa, gym, or conference room. Instead of adding it to that never-ending mental list of queries, I indulge in instant gratification.

"I've noticed The Hotel's stunning workmanship,

especially the doors. There are symbols on the brass plates, but no names. What do they mean?"

Esme's eyes soften, and for a moment, I feel she sees something far beyond me, as though she's peering through time itself, reading something in my future—something I haven't yet lived.

"Symbols were the first language of the soul. Not words," she patiently explains. "Each one holds a vow you've already made, though you may not remember making it. They don't offer meaning or answer questions until you go through the door." She pauses. "I understand you search for logic, as the mind will always seek understanding. Still, it's the heart which recognizes which door is for you when the room and ritual it leads to—and you— are ready." She steps forward, her hand briefly brushing one of the brass plates. "Though Ethan will guide you, you'll know when it's time and where to go. Something with you will call to you. You will be attracted to the design. That same inner voice will answer and guide you, but you need not concern yourself about your journey here. Ethan will assist you.

Perplexed, we stop at a door that's distinct from the rest, yet, I do feel a pull toward it. The brass plate is engraved with a bouquet of peonies—my favorite—and a stunning vein of rose gold runs through the door's wood grain.

"We're here at your suite, Amelia." Esme steps back with a smile. "Welcome. Your journey awaits."

There it is again. That word. Journey.

I fold my arms across my chest, the gesture more instinct than intention, and fix my gaze on her. I'm not sure what to think. When I asked Ethan about that word, the answer he gave still lingers, but remains unsatisfying. I ask again, less harsh than I've asked most of my questions, but no less pointed.

"Why not call it a stay? Why do you, and Ethan, and every whispered word in your carefully curated marketing materials, insist on calling it a journey?"

Esme's expression gentles, though the fire in her eyes doesn't dim. Her demeanor is calm but confident. "Because what happens for a Chosen guest at The Hotel isn't just a stay... it is a journey. Each experience is precisely shaped to meet you exactly where you are... and, hopefully, lead you somewhere you've never been."

A flicker of defiance stirs within me. I don't like being told what to do, and I think I'm just fine the way I am. "What if I don't want to experience a journey? What if I prefer to stay in my room all day, every day, order room service, and do nothing at all?"

"Then, the choice is yours, and you will return to your life just as it was and you were before you accepted the invitation."

Why did that comment just feel like a threat?

Esme turns the handle and pushes open the door, and I don't expect what happens next.

I gasp as I step inside. The beauty of the room is overwhelming, and I fall momentarily speechless. The air inside is warmer than the hallway, and I believe it is the perfect temperature. The air is perfumed with something I can't quite place, but it's a pleasant vanilla scent hovering at the edge of my consciousness.

A rush of pleasure stirs in my chest with something familiar and impossible at the same time. It feels like my mind is straining to remember, and something blooms in me, part recognition but also part ache. I feel like I've stumbled into a forgotten piece of something. I don't know what I expected, but this... this room just feels right. But I didn't. I wasn't asked. And yet, this space reflects me with eerie precision.

A space with all my preferences that would scream luxury and "you deserve this" would look exactly like this. But to capture that in a hotel? It seems almost impossible—and a bit unsettling.

Esme comes up beside me, and strangely, a peaceful feeling showers me. Though she hasn't touched me, her presence steadies me viscerally. "I'll leave you to get settled. If you need anything, Amelia, simply ask."

Her voice is warm, but I detect an undercurrent of surety there. She knows beyond a shadow of a doubt all my needs will be met.

She leaves, and the door clicks shut behind her. Silence settles in—not absence, but something fuller, denser. It fills the room with the soft release of a moment finally unbound. I don't move. I just stand there, letting my senses drink in the stillness. Even my own heartbeat feels loud here, as if it doesn't belong.

My thoughts drift to Esme.

She lingers—not as memory, but as presence. As if a part of her stayed behind to watch. There's something about her I can't quite name. A gentleness that unsettles because it isn't soft—it's precise. Intentional. She looks at me like she already knows. Not what I've done or where I've been—but what I'm trying so hard not to feel. Her voice doesn't soothe. It reaches. And some part of me, no matter how tightly wound, answers. She sees through polish and posture, through the armor I've worn for years, and does so without effort. Her voice doesn't just calm—it resonates like a low note in a song I forgot I knew. And her eyes... they don't look at me. They read me. Her voice doesn't just soothe—it steadies. And her knowing... it isn't arrogance. It's something older. Something earned. If I do nothing else this week, I'm at least interested to learn more about her, this place, and who and what the quote, unquote, "Esme" is all about—and anything else I might discover about The Hotel that I could use to my benefit in the future.

Tossing off business thoughts now that I've made another mental note, I absorb the quiet elegance of the space.

It's perfect.

Soft light filters through beautiful, sheer drapes that billow with lazy movements from an unseen breeze.

They puddle on the floor, looking like an advertisement in a posh decorator magazine. I move toward the window and part the luxurious fabric.

As I gaze outside, my view is so different from the one I see every day. There's no city skyline out this window. No steel or smog. Only an English-style courtyard—lush, orderly, too perfect to be real. Beyond that, mist curls and rolls like a quiet touch through the air, revealing and concealing in equal measure. It moves with purpose, as if guarding something just out of reach.

I lean in, drawn by instinct, not curiosity. Something stirs beyond the haze of white. I squint, straining to focus, when—

A flicker.

The kind that lives at the edge of vision. The kind you feel before you see.

My lungs hitch a beat.

Did someone enter the room while I wasn't looking?

And then—

A chill moves across my skin.

A cold sweep trails behind it, as though the room stirred in response.

Instinctively, my eyes snap toward the movement but see nothing. Not a vent. Not a breeze. Just air that shouldn't be cold, moving across skin that shouldn't feel afraid.

There's nothing there.

Behind the Veil
The Stillness That Recognizes

IN THE QUIET place between Becoming and Memory, Elias stands within the threads of time. He neither moves nor remains stagnant.

He observes.

Not with detachment but with reverence.

The Chosen are not summoned. They arrive when the ache within becomes louder than the accolades. And when they do, Space responds, shivering just slightly, as though her name has been spoken in a tongue older than time.

She, Elias, and others are of The Haven, and the open heart of Juliette awakened them to mortal need.

Now, Amelia has arrived.

The Hotel has waited, not in stillness, but in anticipation. It knows the shape of her footsteps before they touch the marble. It knows her weight, her rhythm, the exact measure of her breath in much the way a violin remembers the bow that once called it to life. Her presence is not disruption.

It is activation.

The Hotel is not silent. It hums beneath her first step inside, alive in a way that cannot be architected or programmed.

It awakens in a new way, now she is inside its walls. Its lifeblood pulses, not as if invaded, but fed. Amelia's precision, control, and poise—these are not obstacles. They are elements. Raw material. Something ancient within the structure recognizes her. A mirror of her tension and potential. A disconnection seeking alignment.

The Hotel is not a building she stumbled into. This is a place built specifically for this woman who does not fall apart but tightens her grip when lines in the world begin to blur.

She is not here to be broken.

She is here to remember.

Already, The Hotel has begun its quiet exchange within its life force. The scent in her suite adjusted the moment she stepped inside with notes of vanilla and something older, something only she would recognize, though she could not yet name. It lingers just beneath her awareness, tugging at a memory she's never fully formed nor lost, a warmth that feels like being held once, long, long ago. Even something seeming so insignificant—the drapes—obeyed her pleasure and gathered themselves to the light in precisely the way she preferred. The silence in the air bent, not emptied, but filled itself, tailored to her need. The Hotel does not demand her vulnerability. It reflects it, backlit and silent, waiting for Amelia to look long enough to see what of her remains beneath the polished veneer.

What Amelia does not yet know is that remembering often feels like unraveling—until it doesn't.

Elias does not judge her resistance or acquiescence. He honors it. He understands the cost of refinement. He sees the care with which Amelia has curated her presence in the world, a quality that is both notable and yet still invisible.

Elias, as the Watcher, sees.

So does The Hotel.

5

It doesn't take me long to get settled, and as soon as I do, I slip beneath the oh-so-comfortable bedding and fall gently, but deeply, into the most restful and unconscious sleep. It folds over me like a soft, warm blanket where dreams blur and shadows shift. When the blackness lifts, I can't tell if minutes or hours have passed.

I shift to look over at the clock and discover I've slept nearly twelve hours. I'm shocked. This is a first for me. I can't remember when I wasn't a light sleeper, and Mother——Mrs. Vivienne Daniels—never let me sleep that long when I was a child, so this feels incredibly indulgent.

Come to think of it, Vivienne Daniels never *let* me do anything. She made me.

I lean back from my curled position, spreading my arms and legs to their full length. I don't want thoughts of my mother to ruin my time away. She chose me when I was three. My parents and I were involved in a deadly car crash. I was the only survivor of a drunk driver's indulgence. A self-made, unmarried woman, she adopted me as a project—proof that she could succeed at any task, especially motherhood.

I push thoughts of her aside, and enjoy a slow, luxurious stretch. When I get out of bed, it meanders through my limbs. I push the curtains aside as moonlight spills through the tall windows. It saturates the room with a peaceful glow.

Arching my back, I turn, relish the unspooling of my body, and take in the peaceful sweetness of the room. Soft hues of blush, cream, and gold wrap the suite in warmth, every element blending seamlessly into the next. The rich, inviting scent of brewing coffee lingers in the air, pulling me from what remains of my sleepy haze, and as I turn toward the suite's entrance, something seizes in my chest. Instantly, my freshly relaxed body turns to stone.

Someone has been in my room.

Breakfast has been laid out, and it's an elegant spread. My body freezes: I stare as steam coils upward from a delicate porcelain cup; the scent that moments ago beckoned me now wraps cold fingers around my spine, sending icicles through my veins.

Pastries.

Ripe fruit.

The arrangement is perfect. Every detail is carefully considered. Every choice was curated with my preferences—except I didn't order breakfast.

And it was brought in while I was sleeping.

Thoroughly creeped out, I fly out of bed. My stomach tightens as I take tentative steps, scanning the room for a person or other signs of disturbance. I check the door. It's locked exactly as I left it when I went to bed. Nothing else in the room is disturbed. No footprints. No shifted curtains. Even the tray— no smudges. There's nothing to prove someone was here, and yet everything suggests they were.

Even the air is still, holding no hint of someone's cologne or perfume mixed with the lovely vanilla.

And yet, someone was here.

I swallow hard, my pulse a steady drum against my ribs. Forcing myself to stay calm is a monumental effort, but I manage to coax my lungs into a slower, more measured pace, looking for anything that might reveal a clue to explain this.

Moments tick by as I scan for clues, but as they pass, I see nothing.

I stare at the tray, looking for a note of explanation. Again, nothing. The silverware gleams in the morning light, offering a distorted reflection of a disheveled me. The napkin is crisply folded beside a plate of my favorites, which waits expectantly for me to devour it. Not just the kind of food I enjoy. The kind I reach for when I'm frayed. When I need comfort but don't want anyone to see I'm unraveling —and the coincidence doesn't seem like a coincidence at all.

I reach for The Hotel's robe, a masterpiece of thick, impossibly soft plush fabric that waits at the foot of the bed. I thrust my arms into the sleeves with urgency. The fabric swallows me. Typically, something so lush would embrace me, but now it feels a sharp contrast to the uneasiness I feel inside. Even the robe feels like a betrayal, soft affection with an agenda.

Anxiety creeps in, unwelcome, as I tighten the sash around my waist. Unease trickles down my spine with a spider-like touch. Apparently, The Hotel exists on its own terms, bending the rules of what's expected and what's explainable. But this? This is unprofessional, creepy, and much too intimate. Though the spread of food is lovely, I no longer feel comfortable or safe.

I won't stay somewhere where I can't have peace of mind.

I reach for the phone. The sleek, pristine design settles into my palm. Then I notice there are no buttons on the base, so I turn it over to inspect the surface for access to room service, front desk, or any other connection before pressing it to my ear, but there are no buttons. No numbers. No dial pad. No options. Just an emblem. A black circle. A golden key. No label. No instructions. Just waiting.

Something crawls beneath my skin.

It's not the lack of options that unsettles me—it's the quiet, deliberate truth behind it. I am cut off. Sealed inside a place that does not need my permission to exist. It does not ask. It simply is.

On instinct, I reach for my phone, clinging to logic like a lifeline.

No bars.

No signal.

Just a blank, indifferent screen that might as well be made of stone.

My throat tightens.

This device, once my symbol of control, now feels like a relic from a world that no longer applies. I toss it onto the bed like it's turned against me, then lift the receiver of The Hotel's phone—half-expecting silence, half-hoping for it. I don't press anything—I can't. As soon as I lift the receiver... she answers.

"Good morning, Amelia." Esme's steady voice fills the receiver.

"Esme, someone was in my room."

"I assure you, no one has been in your room or invaded your privacy, Amelia. You are perfectly safe."

Esme's tone holds not a flicker of concern. Not a moment of confusion. It angers me. Certainty is the last thing I feel.

"I'd like you to come to my room." My tone is stiff. I drop the phone back onto its cradle, not waiting for a response. It wasn't a request. It's an order.

I tamp down the anxiety that threatens to once again rise as I scan the space. My gaze flicks from the corners of the ceiling, then drifts along the wall moldings as I search for a camera. There must be one in here somewhere!

I stalk the room, trailing my fingers along the vanity's smooth surface, the pressure of unseen eyes growing heavier with every step. I peek beneath the mirror and along the frame's edges. Then I move to the bookshelves, running my hands along their spines, then nudging a few aside, my imagination going crazy as I search for a secret room or anything that might prove I'm being watched.

I find nothing.

What about up there?

My head falls back as I lift my gaze to the chandelier and study its crystals. Could some small spying device be hidden? I study them as they sway ever so slightly in the movement of the air conditioning. What is that? I think I see a black dot. Is that a camera?

I quickly drag over a chair and stand on it, moving the glass keys aside and inducing a tinkling sound as they hit together. I tilt my head this way and that way—in any direction to see if that's the source of the privacy invasion, but come up empty.

The dot was nothing.

Just a trick of the light.

Stepping down, I push the chair back into place. My hands unconsciously curl into fists as I cross the room and check near the windows and along the antique table where the breakfast tray sits. The hair at my nape rises as I step back, my heart pounding from a combination of fear and anger. I don't have control of this situation, and I don't like it one bit.

What have I gotten myself into?

I press a hand to my chest, forcing myself to calm down and get control of my emotions. I was caught off guard when I woke. That's why I can't escape this escalation of fear. The anger is valid, and I will express my displeasure and the creeping sense of violation once Esme arrives. I will take note of anything else as I form a plan to confront her, but I need to get my facts straight first. There are no footprints on the plush rug. No sound of a door opening or closing woke me up.

The Hotel is silent, but it is not empty.

The silence isn't passive. It's watchful.

I swallow hard. Whatever this place is, it's watching me, even if I can't see or understand how.

Lowering myself into the chair, my blood runs cold, numbing my fingertips. I reach for the cup of hot liquid. There's no sense letting it go to waste, nor the food on the tray, so I yank a piece of cherry Danish, not taking care of how I do so, and—ouch—some of the hot liquid spills on my hand. Dammit. I shove the Danish in my mouth and quickly set the cup back down, hurriedly wiping my hand against the robe. Quickly, I inspect my skin. No burn. Just a little red.

Slower now, I curl my hands around the porcelain cup, clinging to its borrowed warmth as I chew mechanically as if eating might anchor me to something real. I force myself to draw in air and then let it out with a steady rhythm as I urge my body to settle down. My mother used to say, "Get over yourself, Amelia. You can't control your thoughts, but you can control your reactions."

Then, a knock.

I hurriedly set the cup down. With a severe motion and a rush of anger hitting me like a powerful drug, I again yank the robe's sash. I go to the door, wrench the handle to the side, and pull it open so hard it makes a whooshing sound.

There, Esme stands.

Poised and unshaken, it's as if she's just beyond a touch of the ordinary world, part steward and part ethereal warden of a world I don't understand. She opens her mouth and is about to speak, but I cut her off before she can say a word.

"I'm checking out."

6

"I assure you, Amelia, you are safe." Esme's voice is smooth and warm, carrying the weight of consolation and certainty.

I pause. My thoughts snag and twist like threads pulled too tightly in opposite directions. Each one catches on the next, impossible to follow, impossible to silence. Safe?

The word hovers between us, a fragile thing pretending to be strong, but I don't like it. Not when it's being offered like a gift I didn't ask for. Not when it's handed out like a promise it can't keep.

Once, someone told me I was "safe" right before everything fell apart.

It's not a word I trust anymore.

"My breakfast was waiting for me. I didn't order anything, and I didn't let anyone in."

Esme's gaze holds steady. Her eyes never flicker. There's something about her expression that steadies and challenges me at once. She steps into her presence the way others step into a room.

"The Hotel is a place unlike any other. It is your haven. Every need is recognized and met, and although unconventional by your standards, your safety, needs, and privacy are assured. If your breakfast was waiting, it's because The Hotel recognized and fulfilled your need as you woke."

She says it with reverence, not as a defense but as fact. It's obvious. Sacred. It almost feels like she's offended that I questioned it. Her posture straightens, her chin lifting slightly, and pride flashes across her features.

I stare at her. The words should calm me, but they don't. They sound smooth, rehearsed, and scripted—not to mention unsettling.

"You're making it sound like this place is alive."

"I'm serious in everything I've shared with you," she doesn't hesitate to assure. Her tone never shifts. She gestures toward a nearby chair. "May we sit?"

I hesitate and don't answer immediately. Then I nod. We both take our seats, and I find myself gripping the chair's arms like it might anchor me to something solid.

Just beyond Esme's shoulder, a journal rests on the desk and catches my attention. It's leather-bound and handsome for an old book, but I feel a subtle, magnetic pull to it. The light shining from the window bends differently around it. I dismissed it as décor when I arrived, but now it draws my attention and feels like it might be alert and listening.

"There are things about The Hotel that are easier to understand if you open your mind," Esme explains.

I scoff. "Such as breakfast materializing from thin air? Sounds more like a bedtime story. You know, talking teapots, enchanted candlesticks. I didn't come here for fairy tales."

Her lips curve, not quite amused but undeniably patient. "All I ask is that you suspend the certainty of what you think you know, just for now. The unexplainable happens every day, but most people don't notice. Not because it's rare but because they're too busy denying it. I'm sure you've heard stories about a person's missed exit on the highway that spares a life. A sudden memory of someone gone, followed by a dream, a voice, a sensation that cannot be explained. A melody playing on the radio moments after you think of it."

She's so serious I almost laugh—until I remember the time I thought of my father's favorite song after years of silence and seconds after I thought of him, it played on the airport speakers. I told myself it was a coincidence. But now... between Esme here and Sophie at the office, I have a speck of belief.

"Or how about someone waking up with the impulse to purchase a lottery ticket and then winning? Surely, you've heard stories, Amelia."

I blink. I read something like that just last week. Maybe even yesterday. The thought pulls something loose in my chest. Suddenly, I feel a bit dizzy. My vision tightens, then stretches, as if the room itself is expanding and contracting around me. The edges blur, not with dizziness, but with something more intimate—recognition masquerading as disorientation. A low hum builds behind my ears, not sound exactly, but sensation, like pressure before a storm. My skin prickles. I grip the arms of the chair, fingers tightening until the wood bites back. The shift isn't visible, but it's undeniable.

Something in this room has turned toward me. Or maybe I've turned toward it.

Suddenly, a window opens in my mind, and a memory of someone I haven't thought of in years flickers behind my eyes. And just as quickly, it vanishes.

I blink again, and the dizziness is gone.

Was that me? Or did Esme plant it there?

I clear my throat. "I don't believe in the impossible." My voice is quiet, but there's a slight tremor that I feel and hear.

She waits. Not pressing.

"When did you stop?" Esme's head tilts slightly. "Children believe in the impossible all the time. They imagine freely, without shame. Maybe it's not imagination. Maybe it's clarity. You referenced enchanted dishes, didn't you? Even that metaphor carries a seed of possibility. The mind resists, but the subconscious remembers."

"I think you're putting words in my mouth," I attempt to stay composed. "I was referencing fiction. I deal in facts." My tone is sharper now, a little defensive, and I hate that she can see it.

"Do you?" Esme's voice remains soft, but I hear the thread of challenge. "You discovered us through a vanishing social media post and an emailed invitation that disappeared the moment you accepted. If you're truly interested in facts, how do you explain that? What if something exists between fact and fiction, something unexplainable that's been guiding you all along? Nudging you toward the life you were meant to live, not the one the world told you to build?"

I glance away. I need to dismiss what she's saying, but something in it lingers. The thought makes my heart race, not with fear, but with a sense of recognition.

Esme's voice softens again. "The Hotel is your haven, Amelia. It led you here. It saw what you needed, even before you did."

This is insane. The logical part of me, my whole identity, wants to dismiss everything she's saying. Still, another part, quieter but persistent, wants to believe. Because if anything is possible, then maybe Christian... No. Stop. That's not why I'm here.

"You make it sound like this place knows me better than I know myself."

"It's possible," Esme states the words as easily as someone stating the time.

"But highly improbable," I insist.

"Maybe," she replies, her shoulders moving with a soft shrug. "Then again... maybe not."

Esme stands and walks to the desk. "Join me, please," she requests. I do as asked. She holds out her hand. "May I have your key?"

I hand it to her, and she sets it on the surface.

"If you would, please choose a word that you believe defines you. The first word that comes to mind."

I hesitate. The weight of her request presses deeper than any word should weigh. I glance toward the key. "What if I pick the wrong one?"

"You won't." Her expression is knowing, steady. "The word is already inside you. You just have to say it."

Control. Perfect. Power. Strength. Success. The words roll through my mind, but now, they seem to fit different parts of a persona. Roles I performed. Not truths I lived.

Her presence is steady while everything inside me shifts like sand in a shaken jar. I don't want to say the word that sticks in my mind. Naming it feels dangerous, like pinning myself to a cross I thought I'd climbed down from. But it's the word that made me who I am—or maybe it's the word that kept me from becoming who I was meant to be. But it rises anyway, old and familiar, like the taste of iron in blood.

"Control."

When I meet Esme's eyes, something unreadable flickers in her gaze.

"An interesting choice," her brow quirks. "What does it mean to you?"

"It means everything…and nothing. I was taught it's the only thing that matters," I respond with certainty. "It's what keeps everything neat, tidy, and from falling apart."

She watches me for a long moment. "And if it's the thing holding you back?"

The question presses into me, not like a strike but more like smoke curling under a door. Quiet, invasive, and impossible to ignore.

Esme turns toward the door, her stride as effortless

as when she entered. "It seems the word still knows your name."

The comment wraps around my mind like silk—or a noose. I can't decide which.

The door closes behind her with a soft click, yet her words remain. I look down at the key, and the air shifts. The light bends. My balance falters. When I look again, the metal glints differently. There is an engraving there. Precise. Unforgiving.

Control

A shiver pulls through me. *How the heck..."*

My stomach flips. I have no idea what just happened. The word wasn't there a minute ago and the room feels much different. Charged with energy. It's as if something unseen has been awakened by my admission.

That's when I notice the journal. The leather-bound book that caught my attention earlier is now open. It rests on the desk, and a single page stares back at me, blank but not empty—its surface impossibly soft, almost like it's stirring. The light around it is strange. Dimmer, somehow, but warmer, too, as though it's trying to draw me in without force.

I step closer, and without thinking, I reach out. My fingers barely graze the page when something begins to rise—not appear, not form, but rise. The ink lifts like smoke from beneath the surface, thin at first, like a memory returning after years of silence, then darker, sharper, taking shape.

A scent follows, faint but distinct—charred paper laced with something sweeter, like roses set to burn. I step back slightly, air snagging in my throat. The journal isn't writing itself.

It's remembering.

Juliette Armand,
Countess de Lumière

The 16th Day
The Phase of Stillness
The Time of the Quiet Moon

I do not know what day it is, but when I asked, the measure of time I was given is written above. I do not know where I am, or perhaps I do, but yes, I cannot accept it. My mind wars with my senses, each grasping for dominion over what is real.

The waves carried me here, of that much I am certain. Yet, as I walked upon the shore, my gown torn and clinging to me with salt and sorrow and my body trembling from exhaustion, I find myself in a place that should not exist.

It is too unmoving here. Too still. As if the air itself is holding a long, sacred sentence replacing the terror I felt when the ship wrecked. The atmosphere is almost sacred. Though the circumstance of my arrival was horrid, I feel this place was waiting for me.

Then he appeared.

Elias.

He stood at the edge of the trees, half-shadow, half-sky, watching, not with menace nor pity. Something older lived in his gaze. Curiosity mixed with a kind of unsettling patience. A waiting that did not need to end.

I wanted to run. I should have run. I should have questioned. But instead, I stood frozen, as if the sea had not yet released me. My body betraying my mind's frantic need for logic and control.

"I know you are frightened." His voice was low and knowing as he approached. "But fear and wonder often wear the same face."

I could not answer. My mouth had frozen, and I couldn't shape the words.

I clutched at the edges of my disbelief, desperate to preserve the safety of what I once understood to be real. That is how I have survived, by controlling everything I feel and filtering the world through reason. Breath and bones. That is all I have ever permitted myself to be. A silhouette of a woman shaped into the expectations of others.

Here, in this place, though I cannot explain it, I feel breath and bones are no longer enough.

Elias offers no assurance, no explanation. He simply waits as though he already knew that certainty would be the first thing to unravel within me when truth settles into my chest and something inside me finally opens to it.

And it is.

I feel it unthreading beneath my skin. Curling through my chest as I take in the world around me.

What if, for once, I did not demand proof?

What if I unbuckle the collar wrapped

around my spirit that was so tightly tethered to the expectations of the society in which I was raised?

What if I became something more than the flesh and framework that kept me moving through that world, and I gave myself permission to open to something new? To be a woman no longer enslaved by the skin of her station. To be fully, fiercely, quietly, me.

There is a part of me that I long to explore. The small, long-silenced Juliette wonders if there is a purpose in why I was brought here. Not to escape a drowning death but to awaken the life within me that was never allowed to rise. To unlearn everything I was told was necessary and to experience what it is to live beyond the architecture of expectation.

I am learning there is a difference between quiet and stillness. The first is silence. The second is a presence. And the third is not defined as I have learned. This is Stillness—

the phase they claim belongs to The Quiet Moon.

Perhaps tomorrow, I will demand answers from myself. But tonight, on this sixteenth day of Stillness, beneath the glow of a Quiet Moon I didn't know existed, I will not chase questions. I will rest in the hush of something holy and let the tide that brought me here be enough for now.

In the Stillness,

~ J

7

I pace through the suite, my thoughts as tangled as the ivy carved into the furniture. The journal remains open. Silent now, but no less alive. Its presence lingers in the corner of my vision like something watching—not ominous, just aware. And I'm not ready to admit how deeply I want to read more.

I know I didn't imagine this happening.

I couldn't have imagined it.

I saw it happen right before my eyes. Unbelievable as it might have been, I saw ink rising, blooming across the page like it had been waiting to give me a message. Not written and not simply revealed, but...

the words felt "born." As though they arrived carrying their own purpose.

What the hell is happening?

A slow shiver works its way up my spine. My hand trembles as I reach out again, my fingertips hovering just above the page as if touching it might trigger another impossible event. I've read the words three times now, and still, I don't know what they mean—not fully—but I feel like they see me, and they know me.

Instinct makes me want to bolt. I want to grab my phone, my suitcase, and what's left of my common sense and get out while I still remember who I am. But I don't move. Because there's some part of me—a quieter, buried part—that isn't afraid. It's curious. And I don't know if that makes me more of a lunatic or an explorer.

I pause for a moment to mull over Esme's words. She said The Hotel is my haven. I scoff. Yeah, it is my idea of perfection—although maybe a haunted one.

The thought makes me laugh, but didn't she say I should open my mind? I'm always so logical. So practical. What Esme didn't warn me about was that by considering the impossible, it would feel like my mind was being rewritten from the inside out.

I sink down into the chair and grip the edge of the desk, grounding myself in the rough, real texture of the wood. Curiously, I press my fingers to the journal's page again as if to convince myself that it's just paper, just ink. But it's not. Not anymore. I thought when I came here, I would unwind, refocus, and reclaim the part of myself I thought I'd lost. But maybe I didn't lose her, that girl inside me. Maybe I buried her. If that's the case, and I entertain Esme's explanation about The Hotel, then perhaps this place is digging, not to bury, but to exhume parts of me I thought had died for good.

So, instead of running, and with a long controlled exhale and a resigned sigh, I make the decision to stay. No wavering. I'm sticking to it. Why? Because I need answers. Because I've already stepped into the unknown. And because something inside me wants to believe there's something more to me than what the Board, my employees, and even I have lately seen. I feel like I'm standing at the edge of something vast, something ancient and waiting. The air hums around me here, and though I don't know why, it feels thick with unseen possibility. My heart is racing, and not just from fear anymore, but from the pull of something I don't quite understand, and though I'm unnerved, I refuse to back away.

A knock startles me, pulling me from my thoughts and breaking the silence with the precision of something expected yet not quite desired. I freeze because I'm still a little on edge, with one hand still near the journal and the other clenched at my side. Taking a moment to steady myself before answering, and using those few borrowed heartbeats for courage, I hesitate, but the knock echoes through the space, insistent and too intentional to ignore and also too surreal to trust. I go to move, but my bare feet feel rooted, and I can't. I need that moment to center myself and it feels as if The Hotel eases into the same stillness I'm trying to find. A half measure later, I move.

Pulling on the handle to discover what lies on the other side of the door reveals Ethan standing in the hallway. His linen shirt is open at the collar, and he's wearing a faint smile that softens his chiseled features. He's steady and composed as if he exists entirely outside the chaotic events that most recently wrapped around me.

"Good morning, Amelia." His tone is warm and grounding. "Are you ready for your first journey?"

I place one arm over the other, folding them across my chest. "I'm not sure I'm ready for anything. I have questions. I need answers." I point to the journal. "And, magically, words appeared on the pages of that book, and I didn't write them."

"Ahh. You've met Juliette." His expression softens. There's something about Ethan, something calm and sure, that causes my defenses to falter.

"Yes. Juliette, whoever she is." I issue a hard stare, daring him to make sense of the non-existent woman who bares her soul to strangers through her personal observations and magically rising ink.

He looks over both shoulders into the hallway and then back at me. "Would you like to continue this conversation in the hall, or may I come in?" he asks politely.

With dramatic flair, I sweep my arm through the air, silently granting him permission to enter. He steps inside and walks toward the journal, touches the book, then turns back to me and points toward the chairs in a silent gesture for us to sit.

I don't.

He does.

Ethan leans back and stretches out one leg as if this casual conversation about supernatural things is an everyday occurrence. "First, know that The Hotel selects its guests very carefully," he says. "But I'm sure Esme has explained that to you. Everything here and everything that happens within these walls is designed with purpose. Your purpose. You were selected to come here. To a place designed to fill your soul and senses. The journeys you will take—or rituals, as some call them—are meant for enlightenment. Most especially, they are formulated and designed to help you uncover truths you may not know about yourself."

"And the book? There won't be anything about me in there. Can you explain that? That simply scared the crap out of me." My tone is mildly insistent as fresh goose bumps chill me at the rising of the refreshed memory.

Ethan relaxes further into the chair. "Juliette Armand is the originator of the journeys as we know them. She was the first Chosen at The Haven. If Juliette's words appear in the journal while you are an occupant of The Hotel, she means for you to see them."

"Why?" My brow pinches, and my tone reveals how puzzled and perplexed I feel.

"Because she walked a path like yours in her time," he shares. "What thoughts she imparts may help you to understand better your own journey."

"As I told Esme, I'm not into all the weird stuff."

He shrugs. "Believing or not believing is part of your journey."

"I told Esme I would leave." My tone cuts, but there's hesitation beneath it. I don't want Ethan to know I'm staying to challenge myself. I prefer he suffer a small, unwelcome doubt.

It doesn't rattle him, and he nods thoughtfully. "That choice is always yours, but consider this: you were called here for a reason. Things are happening around us all the time. We may not see them, but they're there. If you choose to stay, I ask only that you keep an open mind. The Hotel doesn't make mistakes. You were brought here because you have something to gain… and something to give."

"That's something like Esme said." I stoop down and lean my hip against the nearby chair, half sitting and half standing, then pull my arms tighter across my chest. "Who are you, Ethan? How did you get here? What's your story?"

A shadow flickers across his face, but he masks it quickly with a gentle smile. "If you don't mind, that's a discussion for another day. For now, my purpose is to guide you and answer questions you may have about your journeys at The Hotel."

His evasion only piques my curiosity. I want to press for details. To demand more, but I have no right to intrude on his life, and something about his sincerity begs me to let it go. I see pain in his eyes, so I decide to take our conversation in a different direction and get his thoughts on an exit plan, should I need one. It isn't that I don't trust Esme, but I need further reassurance that I can leave if I choose.

"About that... my journey... if I decide not to stay after today's 'ritual,' or whatever you want to call it, may I leave with no issues?" I prod.

"The journey for a Chosen is always a choice. Your stay is called a journey, and, yes, while you're here, you will experience some rituals, but they're not nefarious. They are exercises designed to stimulate your thinking. Experiences that will leave you with thoughts to ponder. But as always, your decisions are yours, and we will honor them." His gaze holds a quiet intensity. "But before fear causes you to leave, ask yourself—what was it that brought you here? To this moment? If you didn't want something, if you weren't searching for answers, then why take that first step through the doors? I am absolutely certain that you felt something was different about The Hotel as you approached. When you stepped inside, you felt it even deeper. Everyone does when they discover their vision of a haven."

His words settle over me like dust, soft but inescapable. I look away, the memory of that first moment, the golden light, the strange stillness, the tug I couldn't name, rising like a tide I'd been pretending not to feel.

"I did experience something. I felt a sense of excitement and wonder because this place was exquisite. Still, I was looking forward to a vacation, and this sounds more like a luxury psych test—but I'm staying. At least for now. I've committed myself to being here, and I rarely back away from a challenge."

Determination stiffens my shoulders, and my heart flinches with a speck of fear, but I lock it down. This place may have its games, but so do I. I know how to keep control when everything around me wants to tilt.

I glance over once more at the journal, its open page still glowing faintly with the memory of movement. My pulse stutters, but I straighten. I can't explain what's happening here, not yet, but I won't let it rattle me. Whatever this is, I'm not backing down.

"Okay. Take me to where I need to be, and let's get this over with. Where do I go?"

Ethan's smile widens, patient, yet never smug. "You have a compass to guide you to the chambers meant for you."

I roll my eyes. "No one gave me a compass. Just this." I lift the metal, remembering the word *Control* magically engraved into the shank and what that word means to me.

"The key is your compass. It's been engraved with the first word you chose. It's your guide. It will allow you to enter the rooms that choose you. The Hotel and your key will guide you."

His answer seems to puzzle and toy with me conveniently. I eye the metal in my hand. *A compass?* What am I supposed to do—wave it around like a metal detector?

What are the chambers like? Escape rooms that choose me? This is a little out there for me, like my magically appearing breakfast. I have so many questions, and although I'm convinced there are logical answers, I start a new mental list for these questions. In the meantime, I'll prod just a little. I want to keep Ethan on his toes.

"How will it guide me? A beep? A buzz? How do I know I'm in the right place?"

"I suppose that, too, depends on you. Keep it in your hand as you search for your chambers. I'll walk the halls with you. For some, the key vibrates like a tiny bee. For others, the temperature warms. There is no one set way, but you'll know once you're close to a door, you're meant to open."

"Riiiiigt. "So, I'm playing a grown-up game of hot and cold with a key that reads my soul?"

His brow hikes as his expression lights with quiet amusement. "Something like that. A bit more intuitive than a GPS, perhaps, but yes. The closer you are to a room that's meant for you, the stronger the sensation becomes, whatever form that sensation takes. Some feel drawn. Others feel resistance. Either way, it responds." His voice softens. "And whether or not you enter the chamber is up to you. The choice is always yours, Amelia."

"The word *chamber* sounds like torture, Ethan," I sigh.

"Then call it a room, or a suite... whatever makes you comfortable. This is your journey. If it pleases you to call the rooms and experiences in there something else, you're free to create whatever words you like." His explanation holds the same quiet assurance as Esme's tone.

I narrow my eyes, giving him a sideways glance as my lips press together. I'm not backing out now. My chin defiantly comes up. "Lead the way, Ethan. Let's get this show on the road."

He smiles, amused, and we exit the room together. We wind down one hallway, then another. The key reacts, and a weak buzzing sensation awakens in my palm, making me feel as if we're going in the right direction. I don't know if Ethan is aware of the accuracy of my destination, as I'm not sure who is leading whom. I'd like to think this little piece of metal is giving me control of where we're going, but when I think of my desire for control in even a small situation, such as a walk down a hall, Esme's words about control seep into my thoughts: What if it's the thing that's holding you back?

The thought lodges deep, and I hate how much it echoes. How much it fits.

It's unsettling—how Esme, Ethan, even this place, seem to know me. Not the surface version, but the one beneath—the version I've hidden even from myself.

As we move through the corridor, the air begins to shift. It thickens—not with heat, but with something weightless and pressing, like expectation. The walls feel closer now. Not claustrophobic, just... aware. Watching. Waiting.

I slow my pace. My senses stretch forward, taut as wire. In my palm, the metal stirs—subtle, but growing, its rhythm syncing with something restless inside me. Something I've spent years silencing.

Beside me, Ethan notices. His gaze flicks to the gleaming silver, then rises to meet my eyes. There's something unreadable in his expression that I can only liken to something reverent and knowing.

"We're here, Amelia." His words fall into the charged silence like a stone dropped into still water. Apparently, however the object works, it has done its job.

The door to which the key led me is much taller than I expected. I don't know why that surprises me. I've seen so much grandeur today. Still, something in me pauses. The polished oak gleams beneath its coats of lacquer, the grain warm under the corridor's soft light. Almost as if it's radiating heat toward my palm. At its center, a brass plaque catches the glow. A mask is carved into it. One side is smooth, the other fractured by a fault line that runs down the middle. It's as if the façade of perfection has split. The cracks on that side spider out in jagged lines, each pointing toward an exposed core. I swallow, realizing it reminds me of the faces I've worn. The ones covered with makeup and forced mindsets that splintered the moment I pushed too hard. There were many times I was expected to be something—or someone—that wasn't me. I pause. Tell myself it means nothing to me. That I'm looking too hard for meaning in an inanimate object. *But it isn't nothing.* The plaque hums with awareness, and the faint vibration skims across my skin, making the fine hairs on my arms rise.

"This is the Chamber of Reflection," Ethan announces. "If you're meant to enter this room, what's in your hand will unlock the door."

"Are you going in with me?" I ask.

He shakes his head. "No, Amelia. This is your journey, and what happens within this room is meant specifically for you."

8

I pull air slowly into my chest, deep, measured, and controlled, and press my lips into a determined line. The confirmation of Ethan's absence within this "chamber" settles like a stone in my chest. Am I afraid of what's inside? Maybe. But mostly, I'm irritated. He said he was my guide, and perhaps I clung to that word too tightly, mistaking it for accompaniment instead of instruction. Of course, I'm doing this alone. I knew that. They told me that. I just didn't want it to be true.

Lingering at the door, I conform my hand to fit the cool brass handle and take a brief moment. I wonder why I'm even doing this. If the choice is mine, as Ethan and Esme say, I could be in my room, in bed, wrapped in crisp sheets, ordering room service, and losing myself in a book instead of losing parts of myself to whatever this crazy place demands. So, why am I pressing myself to go in?

Because you're not a quitter, that's why.

The internal monologue stops as the door swings open with an almost imperceptible sigh. Ethan steps back, and I feel the space between us chill as I move forward.

As I step inside, the door clicks behind me, and the air folds inward. The sound is too soft for drama but too sharp to ignore. It doesn't feel like it's just closing. It feels more like it's sealing me in.

I quickly shut down a claustrophobic prick as the floor vibrates beneath me with a barely there thrum. It feels like a warning from somewhere deep inside my brain, lying below rational thought. The chamber illumination rises and dimly lights what's before me. The room is lined with mirrors that rise like monuments. Their frames curl toward the ceiling, solemn and watching. Between them, delicate ovals nestle like secrets while slender full-length panes lean at odd angles. It's as if they've grown weary of standing straight. Sharp-edged fragments of reflective glass are scattered along the walls like broken echoes of something long forgotten. A few of the mirrors are clouded, their surfaces silvered and ghostly like mercury glass. At the same time, others gleam too brightly, bending the golden light and distorting it as it fractures reality into a thousand versions of itself.

My nerves shake me inside as I'm not sure what to think. The air is heavy and charged. Thick with something unseen. A shiver trails down my spine and embraces me, pressing against my back like a ghostly hug. There's a haunting whispering along my senses.

These walls have eyes.

I move cautiously toward the reflective glass, their surfaces shimmering not just with my present image but with versions of me I'd forgotten. Me as a child. As a teen. At college graduation. Standing beside the first car I bought.

I don't know how this is happening, but these aren't just reflections; they're witnesses. Fragments of a life I lived, which, at times, felt never-ending, yet became those memories I pushed to the back of my mind, allowing myself only a brief pause to inhabit them.

This room isn't just strange; it unsettles my balance. I feel like I'm stumbling into spaces of time I never meant to revisit. They follow me with their history and the weight of something unfinished. Truths I've locked away for years.

I move forward again, and this time, the air doesn't shift. The room is still as bone, and when my gaze finds itself in the mirror, so am I.

My pulse leaps as my reflection smiles at me while I do not. Its lips curve into a grin, and a voice that sounds like mine but isn't slips from its mouth, calm yet unnatural and slightly distorted, as if it's been waiting too long to speak. As I stare, I realize my first impression was wrong. It's not a grin. It's recognition. Possession. As if some part of me I exiled is stepping forward to reclaim its face.

"Welcome, Amelia. Do you know who you are?"

A chill ripples down my spine. I felt the subtle yet undeniable shift in this room the moment I entered, and now I am confident that there is another presence here. The room had paused, suspended, as it waited for me to enter. Now, though I can't explain it, it seems to move again—and that shift curls around me. Not demanding. Just inevitable.

The future caught up to a secret the past never stopped whispering. The Chamber called for this version of me, and I answered, choosing to stand before whatever secrets it's been guarding in the dark. Somehow, that makes it feel more dangerous and more real.

The floor below me shifts, not enough to make me stumble but enough to tell me something beneath it has awakened. A deep groan snags my attention as it hums through the structure as if the walls have old bones and are just now remembering how to stretch. I steady myself and move forward as the air presses around me, swelling with something I can't name. It clings to my skin like mist, threading beneath my sweatshirt. It isn't cold but feels... curious.

"Who's here?" I ask the room. Though my voice is level, there is a tremble in my hands. I rotate slowly, scanning the space, my eyes flicking toward every subtle movement, my skin prickling at each faint shift of air that brushes across my arms. The silence is too quiet. Too cinematic. Like it's waiting for a first scream.

Out of nowhere, the scent in the room changes. It

isn't gradual. It arrives like a ghost of something half-remembered, intimate, and uninvited.

Summer storms on a front porch.

The charged hush before rain.

The sun-warmed pavement beneath scraped knees.

These are mine. Not hers. Mine.

And then something sour—familiar. A perfume worn by someone I trusted for too long. It clings like betrayal.

My throat tightens before I know why. These scents don't just trigger memory. They excavate it. And for a moment, I am young again, sensing danger behind the lullaby of safety.

That terrifies me more than I care to admit.

I move, and the chamber drinks in my presence, adjusting to my hesitance with eerie grace. It senses the weight I carry, what I've tucked away and ignored for years, and it waits. It knows the truth: I've spent a lifetime managing beneath achievement and strategy. I can feel it.

I've always felt things I shouldn't have. Always seen beyond what I could explain. But Mother taught me to disregard those instincts, to stop being sensitive, and to shape myself into something more acceptable. More reliable. Something impressive. A person in control.

A breeze glides across the back of my neck, gentle and deliberate. There's no visible source. Still, I know I'm not alone. I've always known. Despite my explaining everything away with logic and pooh-poohing away comments Sophie makes about the supernatural, deep down, I know there's something in me I can't explain. Even as a child, I sensed it. My grandmother—Mrs. Daniels's mother—called it "the presence behind the Veil." Vivienne never hit me—not with hands—but with expectations sharp enough to scar. She didn't want a daughter. She wanted a reflection. And every time I saw things she couldn't explain, things she refused to believe, she looked at me like I'd failed her. Stop imagining things, Amelia. As if wonder was a flaw. As if knowing—really knowing—was something to be ashamed of.

Vivienne's mother—"Grandmère," as Vivienne insisted I call her—was softness and wild violets. She smelled like ginger tea and old books and always let me speak without interruption. She believed me when I said I felt things. Of course, you do, ma petite, she'd whisper, her voice like rain on parchment. The women in my line have always sensed what others silence, and I detect it in you. Most women can sense the emotions of others, but some who've grown hard shut down that part of themselves. Though you are not my blood relative, I believe every woman has the gift.

After she died, that part of me became inconvenient. Mother didn't like it.

Vivienne tried to shame it out of me. Tried to polish the edges until nothing strange remained. And when that didn't work, she ignored it. Ignored me. I learned to stop sharing and to smile when I wanted to scream.

Eventually, I made myself easier to praise.

Easier to claim.

Something shifts within the walls—too soft to see, too sure to ignore. Not cold. Not threatening. A warmth, slow and sure, opens nearby like silk shifting from a gentle touch. It doesn't move toward me. It simply exists. Steady. Luminous. A presence without form, watching—not as a warning, but as a welcome.

It doesn't intrude.

It waits.

And somehow, I know... it's been waiting a long time.

A name surfaces in my mind's eye without warning.

Lysander.

I don't know how I know it, only that it belongs to the warmth around me and is an entity I cannot see but whose existence I feel is beyond my comprehension. Its presence wraps around the space like a silent vow.

The mirrors flicker, and my gaze skips from one to the other, looking for someone named Lysander. Their glass doesn't reflect the present, and the versions of me they hold begin to shimmer with moments long buried. A little girl, hands folded too tightly in her lap. A teenager smoothing the edge of a paper marked with an A. A woman in a tailored suit, spine straight, arms crossed like a fortress.

"You are afraid," a voice deep, calm, and unyielding states the truth. It isn't cruel or mocking.

I jump. "I'm not afraid of you," I bite out. The lie tastes sharp in my mouth, like bitten brass.

Although I tell Lysander I don't fear him, I am afraid of what he may make the mirrors show me.

No one answers. But the mirrors ripple. The child smirks. "I'm not afraid of you," she parrots my own voice, mocking me. The other versions of me echo her, their voices overlapping in a chorus too familiar—mocking, sharp, merciless in tone. They don't shout. They don't scream. They taunt—like doubt curling its fingers around a fragile truth.

My heart hammers, each beat a warning. But I don't move.

I won't.

"I'm not afraid of anything," I whisper, then louder, firmer as if saying it makes it real. "I built a life from discipline and determination. I turned silence into strategy. Sacrifice into success. I didn't inherit anything—I became something."

But the words falter, heavy in my mouth.

They don't ring true.

They clang.

The truth stirs—metallic and sharp—as the taste of the lie coats my tongue. Not bitterness.

Recognition.

A mirror fissures.

Not with a crash, but with precision—like a hairline fracture in something once thought unbreakable. Another splinter chases it, then another. The sound is delicate but final.

The room no longer believes me.

And neither do I.

The fissures spiderweb outward and the room pulses with pressure. Another voice, this one deeper, smoother, arrives like a shiver slipping beneath my skin.

"There is no shame in fear," he says. "Only discovery."

The comment burrows into my chest, not loud, but undeniable. There is weight to his words, and they feel like something ancient pressing against my soul.

Though I know the answer to my question, I demand confirmation. "What is your name?"

"I am called Lysander."

"What is your purpose, and what do you want from me?"

"I am The Keeper of Origins. The one who remembers what came first. The one who chases the forgotten, the erased, the unspoken beginning of all things. I am the Architect who never stops searching for what the others deem lost."

"Architect? Architect of what?" I demand.

"I am but one of many. We are the unseen hands that guide what was and encourage what will be. We do not rule, and we do not command. We remember. We weave. Each of us guards a principle, an elemental truth that shapes the arc of becoming. Some build. Some watch. Some bear light into the dark. I help humankind in their search. For what was lost. For what they no longer believe can be found."

"You cannot hurt me," I announce. "I was assured I would be challenged but not harmed." The slight tremble in my voice exposes me.

"I will not hurt you." He confirms.

I quickly scan the room, searching for a form of something—of him—but finding nothing. "Why can't I see you?"

"My presence resides beyond the Veil, hidden from human eyes."

"The Veil?" I ask. The word tastes foreign—ancient and intimate at once.

His voice lowers, like a memory speaking itself aloud:

"It is not a wall, Amelia. It is forgetting. Not the kind that comes with time, but the type that's chosen. When the truth is too loud to bear, when grief carves too deep, when a child learns that silence is safer than being seen... a veil is born.

You've passed through it a thousand times—each time you swallowed your voice, each time you smiled instead of screamed. It does not hide what is gone. Only what you're not yet ready to remember."

The air stills. I feel it—not with my skin, but somewhere older, somewhere beneath logic. The Veil isn't just a cosmic mystery.

Lysander's presence doesn't intrude and doesn't feel threatening. He is silent while the mirrors once again shift. They no longer show moments. They show truths.

The child I was, sobbing silently into a pillow. The teen who turns away, pretending to be asleep as a single tear trails down her cheek. The woman, smiling in the mirror, her eyes vacant, her heart breaking.

Each version holds the shape of a wound I didn't quite know how to name but bandaged, only to have the protective layer ripped off over and over again.

"Have you built a life?" He gently asks. "Or have you erected a prison?"

I close my eyes for half a second, trying to steady my shaking legs as memories rush in. Though I try to brace myself against the hit, they unmoor me from any semblance of control. The question's grip is also felt by the room. The mirrors groan, strained beneath the weight of the past I refuse to admit. Before I can steady myself and muster an answer to Lysander's question, the temperature drops to an icy depth.

Someone else is here.

9

The air stills—no longer watchful but waiting. The warmth that surrounded me retreats to the edges like a tide pulling back, and in its wake, a different presence arrives. One I don't trust.

Something in the air slithers up my spine. A menace dressed in silk. It smells like endings, ashes, and regret, like the last page of a story you wanted to finish. Like lipstick on an envelope, you were never meant to open.

As with Lysander, the second presence enters the room, uninvited and unannounced. But this one feels different, and the cold seeps into my chest like frost under the door of a locked room. I think its identity and its name comes to me on a hiss.

Vesper.

"You don't want change, do you, Amelia?" The voice slinks into my mind like a velvet glove lined with razors. Feminine and silken. Soft and devastating. It's too smooth to trust. It doesn't speak as much as coo, every word stretched and curved, vowels drawn out like a sigh through red lips, and consonants sharpened like claws. It wraps around the edges of my mind like velvet soaked in poison—lush, seductive, and laced with ruin. I can't see her, but I feel her. She's not near. She's inside. Threading herself through my thoughts like a lover slipping into a dream.

"You've worked so hard to become who you are," she whispers, the words sliding in like a blade hidden in lace. There's no kindness in her tone—only the performance of it. "Why unravel now? Why risk becoming less... just to feel more?"

The mirrors shudder in their frames, and something in me does, too.

I step back without meaning to. My lungs hesitate. My eyes cut across the room like knives trying to find what they already know is here. My pulse ticks faster. Not from fear of her—but from recognition of the war she's trying to start inside me.

"Are you also an Architect?" I demand.

"Me?" She laughs deeply, then discharges a dramatically indulgent exhale. "No, A-meeel-ia." She draws out my name like pearls through a grave. "The Architects build. They want you to excel and build. They want you to chase stars and dream dreams." A pause. "So exhausting," she mutters. "I am what you enjoy. The Shroud that covers you when you sit still."

A beat passes, but my disbelieving mind begins to compute that I'm in a room with two entities I cannot see, yet am conversing with. My rational is blaring that tells me this is absurd, while my gut is telling me I'm at a point of reckoning while they play tug of war with my mind.

"I asked if you were an Architect," I repeat.

"And I mentioned I was a Shroud—though we have not been easily named. We do not reveal potential or what can be. We reflect on what is. We do not push you through complacency. We gently whisper. We do not bother." Her voice drops lower; the velvet tone wrapped in smoke. "We are the cool that kisses out the fire. The comfort that softens the truth until it no longer matters. We are the stillness beneath ambition. The comfort in surrender. We are the magnificent force that keeps the world calm while burying their nerves. We cradle the world in forgetfulness because remembering hurts too much, doesn't it, Amelia? And so, our name is fitting. I am—and others like me—are the Shrouds."

"Shrouds?" The word scrapes the inside of my throat, and something primal and wrong spills inside me. My lips burn and taste like ash from a fire long extinguished but never forgotten. A shudder rises in my chest before I can stop it, and my beating heart races. I don't know what they are or if they're real. This could be a special effect or a mind trip at The Hotel. The possibility of a hallucinogen in that bite of Danish scores a question in my over-circuiting thoughts. What I am sure of is that Vesper's name alone has coiled around my ribs while I was gathering information. The grip is tightening with a cold and suffocating chill.

"The Shrouds seduce," Lysander voices as if trying not to wake something sleeping. "They infiltrate the cracks within truths. Once inside, they do not take; they replace, and you find a place within you to tuck away the event, its facts now corrupted."

The mirrors still. Every version of me—young, old, smiling, breaking—freezes their gazes, locking onto mine with eerie patience. Somehow, I detect that they know the naked facts of my life, the times they represent. It's creepy and unsettling, and because I get the feeling they remember things I might not, the only one left out of this game is me.

"State your name!" I demand, kicking into CEO mode to hide how unnerved I am.

"Vesper."

The sound of her name slithers through my mind like a venomous cancer. It's silent and searing, the bitterness of acid in the mouth.

Silence reigns uncomfortably, and my pulse ticks a racing beat. I feel like I'm being pulled, and, despite my efforts at strength, like a thread, I'm unraveling in slow motion.

"She is Vesper. The Dagger of Doubt." Lysander's voice steadies me as it slices through the air. "We are not the same, Architects and Shrouds. Our missions are not equal. Architects appeal to your vision of what can be. Shrouds absolve you of any ambition to create it."

"But how? I don't fit that mold. I am a very accomplished woman." I ask.

"They dress fear with elegance. We temper fear with sheer truth. They absolve you of ambition. We remind you of the mountain you were born to climb. They allow you the grace to fall. We challenge you to then rise."

His voice is solid and cuts clean. There's no malice in it, only truth spoken with the sorrow and heavy ache of someone who has seen many falls while hoping they would rise. Within Lysander's tone, I hear the weight of memory. Of history repeating itself. Of warning dressed as fact, yet dismissed."

The temperature, though not warm, had risen as he spoke. Now, a chill, once again, rides the air.

"Tsk. Tsk. Tsk." Amused, Vesper clicks her tongue. "You make us sound so bad, Lysander." She chides.

I feel it, then. Not just Vesper and Lysander, but a collective presence. As if the others they speak of linger just beyond the edge of what I can see.

Something in my chest stutters. "I don't know who's here and needs to hear me state the words, but—I have risen, and I have climbed!"

"Have you?" Lysander interjects. "Or have you only scaled the walls built to keep you from yourself?"

His tone is calm and doesn't challenge me, but it weighs heavily on my heart. It reflects. There is no conviction within his tone, only the weight of a truth long carried. One which he offers me with careful grace.

His words fold into a space in my mind that feels like a memory returning.

"We have watched, Amelia. You have achieved much. But at what cost? What did you silence inside yourself to be heard by others? "What did you give of yourself, not out of love, but because success felt safer than vulnerability?"

The mirrors ripple. Their shifting surfaces flicker. Versions of myself I'd long buried look at me with a plea to remember the girl who once painted barefoot in the sun and the woman who once believed joy didn't have to be earned.

"To rise is not the same as to become," he states in a quiet voice. "And to climb is more to push yourself to fit into a space; it isn't the same as offering the world the gift with which you were born. The one you were sent to share." He pauses, and the truth of it lands sharp in my chest. "You have reached the summit, yes. But did you carry your whole self with you or bring only the fragments you believed the world might accept?" A heavy, intimate silence grows, allowing me to soak in his words before he once again offers his thoughts. "You gave everything demanded of you—but what haven't you given yourself?"

Shaken, I look into the mirror at myself. The accomplished version of myself. For a moment, I don't know who she is. Not exactly. I know the feeling of her. The cool logic she possesses and worships. Her calculated poise. She's the woman who adapts, so she seems familiar in any scene, but is she true? I've been obeying her all my life. Not necessarily because I wanted to, but because I thought I had to.

"Change is hard—and you don't want to change, do you, darling?"

Vesper croons, startling me from my introspection. Her question slithers through my mind as warm as stolen heat.

The walls once again come alive, and The Reflection Chamber hums. I look into the mirrors, and they warp, but hesitate; their silvered depths seem to quiver as they wait, uncertain.

"Why do you need to change, Amelia?" Vesper purrs, the inquiry thick with promise and sweet with decay. "Haven't you worked hard enough?"

Her words echo within, then settle, sliding into cracks I've pretended aren't there. Though there is silence, Vesper's voice is everywhere inside of me.

"You fight. You push. You control. It doesn't matter if you're using the talent you were born with or the one you carved out of stone." She pauses for effect, and it has one on me. As I soak in her words, pride rises up within me, complete and powerful like a raging storm. She sighs. "You know what it's given you. You don't have to dig up a life mission that might not serve you as well."

A chill rolls over my skin, this time not from fear but recognition. I've clung to control like a life raft. Like armor. Like truth. "Who I am has given me everything I've ever wanted."

The mirrors tremble with force. My reflection is no longer the me I used to be. A version I admire stares back. Colder. More rigid. Stiffened spine and calculated gaze, daring the mirrors to show me as I am.

I shake off the anxiety and fear with which I entered this room. As I look at myself, I see I'm every inch the woman who clawed her way through boardrooms and constructed buildings out of broken expectations. The me who refused to bend. But there's something in her azure depths I haven't formally detected.

When I look into her eyes, they're hollow.

"Efficient. Perfection. In control," Vesper praises. "That's what you are, Amelia—and that is who you'll remain.

One mirror morphs, showing me as a child—bright-eyed, messy, curious. Then older, polished, poised, spine like steel. I barely blink as her icy blue gaze locks onto mine. She's powerful. But hollow.

Vesper chuckles, the sound sinfully sweet. "Who would you be if you paid attention to thoughts like Lysander's?" Her voice lowers, the silkiness caressing my skin. "Softness hasn't gotten you to where you are?"

The scent hits before I realize what it is—rich, sharp, unmistakable. The perfume I wore the day Forbes interviewed me. Exotic. Luxurious. A blend I chose with care because I knew what message it sent. It cost me a month's salary, and I didn't flinch. I deserved it. I earned it. That fragrance wasn't about vanity—it was a declaration. Power has a scent, and that day, I wore it like proof. Kindness didn't get me the invite. Compassion didn't close the deal. It was discipline. Control. Performance. The things I mastered to survive and to succeed. And now, standing here with that same perfume curling into the air, I remember exactly who I became to get where I am.

The mirrors react, groaning under the weight of the memory. A sound like strained wood or old bones shifting. Pride presses against the glass like a storm at the door, and Vesper's silence feels like applause. A crack ripples the glass.

"Bend, and you might break." Vesper's words kiss my skin, seducing my pride even further. A seed has been planted, and its whisper lingers beneath ambition's roar.

I can't be soft. It corrodes. I entertained the board's request, edict, but why? Why should I change?

"You have control. "Vesper lets out a faint, serpentine whisper, the words brushing my ear like a soured lover's murmur. "You don't need to surrender to anyone's wishes but your own. You're the one in control—and control is perfect."

Both words slip beneath my skin and thread through my bones. I feel Vesper's grin. I was taught to strive for the brass ring. The gold star. To control any task I was given and to perform the actions perfectly.

Controlled.

Perfect.

But... what if I don't want to be?

"Doubt is never loud, Amelia. It whispers until it rules." Lysander's words tighten the air around us, and the chamber closes in.

Shadows dance across the mirrors. They twist, refract, and replicate. A dozen eyes blink from a dozen surfaces, all fixed on me. Some amused. Some bored. Some simply reaching for me as if to pull me inside. Their expressions slip between my thoughts and thread through my ribs, anchoring in a hollow where a part of self-doubt bloomed.

Suddenly, sensations overwhelm me, causing me to turn this way and that. A shift in the air too subtle to name. A ghost of a touch at the curve of my spine.

The trace of something bodiless that knows exactly how to reach me.

The mirrors inhale. The space between them folds in. Their edges bend and ripple, and the glass shivers, restless and angry. Watching. Waiting.

"No, doubt is never loud, Lysander—but pride screams."

Vesper laughs, sounding like spun sugar mixed with venom. The mirrors shudder. More reflections appear. Me, in my finest moments, polished and poised. As a child, wide-eyed and wondering. And exhausted, fingers clenched. Holding myself together.

Then, silence.

Nothing.

Their faces vanish, blank voids where I should be.

Suddenly, screams split my ears. I cower, covering them with my hands as voices cry out from the empty mirrors. Desperate ones I've abandoned.

"Help us! Help us! We want to be seen!"

Their pleas are in different octaves and shake me to the core. A child's wail. A teenager's cry. A college girl's lament. I shiver as their screeches fill the air. The emptiness is heartbreaking, but it's the erasure that steals my control—and Vesper notices.

"Oh, dear Amelia," Vesper laments. "You don't know which version of you is real."

With a volcanic rush, rage presses upward from a place inside. A place I didn't know existed. Hotter. Heavier. Something I've contained for years beneath polished smiles and perfect plans.

My fingers curl into a fist—tight, aching, trembling. My voice burns at the back of my throat, ready to shatter something sacred.

Defiantly, I lift my chin. My heart thunders in my chest, and my blood simmers with rage.

"I know exactly who I am!"

The air cracks with the sound of something ancient breaking loose, and at the same time, something inside me fractures.

"We're done here!" I roar.

The moment the words fall from my lips, the mirrors explode. Glass rains around me like the sky itself cracked open. I don't shield myself. I watch the shards fall.

Behind the Veil
The Fracture Before the Break

TIME DOES NOT PASS HERE. It waits.

Beyond marble halls and mortal memory, there is a space not bound by doors, only thresholds. It exists behind the Veil, a realm between the known and the unknowable, where silence is a living thing, and light bends without source or shadow. The floor beneath is not stone but memory itself, woven from air and ash and the remnants of truths never spoken aloud.

It is not a place one can enter. It is a place that watches, that bears witness. It is the hush between heartbeats, the pause before a soul turns toward itself.

Here, the air trembles.

Elias stands at the edge of Becoming, where endings release and beginnings take their first shape.

A presence stirring.

A reckoning rising.

"She's angry," Elias notes, the words as heavy as thunder.

The Hotel hears, feels, and senses Amelia's rage with interest. The disturbance is noted. Paintings along empty corridors tilt on their hooks. Candle flames flicker, though no wind moves them. Beneath the floorboards of her room, heat pulses in steady waves. She does not know she is being absorbed—but it is constant.

Vesper forms near Elias in a slow spiral of smoke and shadow, her figure coalescing as if born of the Veil itself.

"I know, Elias," she murmurs, her voice warming deceptively with something like delight. "But rage is just fear dressed for war." A curl of her lips. "We'll meet again."

She turns, dragging one finger through the air until it sings, and far below the realm in which she resides, Amelia flinches, unaware of the ripple across her soul.

Lysander stands opposite, grave and radiant in the way only truth can be. He does not flinch or blink. Vesper plays her part just as he plays his.

His eyes are fixed on the hairline fractures appearing in the polished veneer of Amelia's restraint.

"I prefer the illusion fall," he states. Each word lands with weight, like a tolling bell. "Let what's false shatter so what's real can rise."

And shatter it does.

The Hotel responds. Somewhere, a lock snaps without warning. A light extinguishes itself, forsaking the beauty it once revealed.

Vesper tilts her head, admiring the unraveling as if it were a painting in motion. "Amelia breaks so beautifully," she purrs.

Lysander does not look at her. His gaze holds the hairline fractures in Amelia's restraint. "No," he says quietly. "She begins." The Veil shimmers between them, as thin as silence, vast as memory.

For a long moment, the four remain. Elias. Lysander. Vesper.

And the presence that is The Hotel itself.

Each aware. Each listening. Each feeling the rhythm of transformation taking hold.

Elias's silence affirms the truth: this was always the path. The anger. The resistance. The desperate clinging to what was never meant to last. Amelia is not being punished. She is being invited. Coaxed to find what is within.

As her emotions rise and fall, The Hotel adjusts. Rooms reconfigure behind her back. Hallways narrow. The air thickens with knowing. She will not understand until later that the sound she called rage was her soul finally waking from its slumber.

Vesper fades, but her laughter lingers, stitched into the atmosphere like perfume that refuses to lift.

Lysander stays, one hand pressed lightly to the unseen barrier that divides their world from hers. "She will try to rebuild the facade," he says softly. "They always do."

Elias inclines his head, barely a nod. "And she will fail."

Lysander's gaze does not shift. It challenges. "Until she doesn't."

He goes, and the Veil dissolves as midnight folds itself around the edges of becoming a thousand watchful stars blinking through the dark.

And Elias confidently waits, for what may break Amelia is not the end.

It's the beginning she has always feared.

And far below, though she does not yet know it, Amelia is making a choice. Every quiet pause. Every resistance. Every crack in her certainty is a prayer for what waits behind the Veil.

10

My room is a storm in motion. Drawers slam. Fabric snaps with frantic movements. My hands shake as if the gale rages inside of them.

I yank clothing from hangers without thinking, my lungs pulling air in, the inhales sharp and uneven. Thinking is an impossibility as my heart pounds in an erratic, frustrating rhythm. There's something else there, too. Something deeper that's been exposed. Something I can't, or won't, name.

The pressure in my chest is nearly unbearable and builds like a rising tide, pressing hard against my ribs. I feel caged, frantic. This feeling of needing escape is so overwhelming. I don't know what I'm trying to escape from or where I'll go; I just know I need to run. I don't know if I'll call a car or just walk until the weight in my chest dissolves. I just need out.

A knock sounds, which I barely hear over the pounding in my ears. "Come in!" The words snap from my constricted throat, brittle and jagged.

The door opens, and Esme steps inside. I freeze, and my shaking hands drop to my sides.

She wears her concern well, as it seems she does most expressions. She is everything I'm not—poised, grounded, and calm. A pillar of gravity in my unraveling chaos.

"Amelia..." Her voice is a plea, steady and low. I don't know what it is about her, but a hum of calm wraps around the chaos, softening it just a bit.

Despite the anxious feelings and the bid for me to continue my escape, my shoulders drop.

"I can't stay here, Esme." The words rush out, desperate and too loud. Too pathetic. "This place, this... Hotel, it's too much for me. That was too much. I didn't sign up for that."

She watches me, not with pity or amusement, but with that almost maddening, gentle patience that seems to be her way. "And yet, something in you did."

"And soon I'll be gone." The response is immediate, and I feel the warmth of anger flicker once again.

Esme comes before me, her hands clasped. "Even if you didn't understand why, something called to you from The Hotel, and you answered."

I scoff, stand up straight, stiffen my spine, and fold my arms tightly across my chest. "Well, I made a mistake."

"Did you?" Her head tilts slightly, not in challenge, but more in a knowing way. "Your intuition led you here, and you have completed your first ritual journey. What you've learned through it might not be entirely clear now, but revelation doesn't always occur instantaneously."

The weight of her calm irritates me and makes my skin itch. I'm usually the one composed, and the fact that I'm not makes me shift uncomfortably. "I didn't come here to have my mind messed with. I don't know what that was in your Chamber of Reflection," the title bitter as I employ the use of air quotes, "but it wasn't fun, and it sure as hell wasn't relaxing."

"And, again, you've completed your first ritual. I assure you, what happened within the Chamber wasn't for effect." She pauses. "The experiences you have while here aren't meant to harm you. They're meant to reveal what you've been hiding from yourself." Her voice lowers, like a secret slipping into the air. "And what may be hindered in that regard, disguising as something else. The Architects and Shrouds—"

"Stop!" My pulse spikes.

The Shrouds.

The title lands heavy. I don't know what my body's trying to tell me, not really. But something in me recoils. My jaw clenches, and my shoulders stiffen. "Are they another one of your cryptic, mystical things because I met one of them, and if so, I'm out." I throw up my hands, the sarcastic tone sharp as I try to reclaim control the only way I know how.

She steps closer to me.

"Amelia. Please sit for just a moment."

I hesitate, but the look in her eyes begs me to comply, so I plop onto the bed with the dramatic defiance of a child, arms still folded, every muscle tense.

Esme lowers herself into the chair across from me with that same infuriating grace. She looks like she could sit there for a hundred years and not grow tired. I can't tell if her expression is one of pity or unshakeable calm, but my guess is a mix of the two.

"When The Hotel invites or calls, if you prefer, there are ancient forces at work."

I let out a sharp laugh. "Forgive me, but bullshit."

She doesn't flinch and stays focused on her message. "The Hotel is a modern-day extension of another place, The Haven; it's governed by forces. They exist beyond our realm but respond to an unspoken call of the Chosen. You may not realize it, but The Hotel is your creation. Somewhere, deep inside of you, you have a vision of a perfect place for you to escape. This place, The Hotel, was created with you in mind. It shifts with your essence and indulges your imagination."

I blink. That's absurd. And yet... something in me bristles—not with disbelief, but recognition.

"Entities who exist beyond this realm, beyond the Veil, have their place at The Haven. They have for centuries. They are called The Architects of Eternity and The Shrouds of Oblivion, or, if you prefer, the

Architects and the Shrouds, for short. They're forces woven into existence itself, older than memory and fear and more powerful than either of us. When a Chosen accepts an invitation from The Haven to a place created from their desire, those Architects and Shrouds assigned to the Chosen dwell within the Chambers."

For a second, I stare, dumbfounded. Then, a huffed laugh escapes. "Right," I mutter. "So this place is... what? A cosmic Air B&B I never booked, run by mystical staff? A magical rental customized by my subconscious?" I bark a laugh, but it comes out too thin and brittle. "That's... that's rich, Esme."

As the words leave my mouth, I feel the tremor beneath them. But I remember the ink rising on Juliette's page—how it knew me. How it spoke to the part of me I tried to drown in ambition. I felt seen in a way that left me raw.

And the mirrors... they remembered things I've tried to forget.

I want to believe this is a dream, a delusion, or some twisted therapy experiment with excellent set design. And yet...

Something in me knows the truth, and I don't like it. Some strange feeling in my gut is telling me Esme isn't lying, and that's the part I fear the most.

She smiles softly. "There are things in this universe no one can explain, and to believe we understand it all, to think it's all limited to this little planet, that's arrogance, in my opinion. The Hotel exists for its Chosen and to help you find the parts of you that have forgotten who and what you were born to be. When you are chosen, it's because your Haven and the Architects and Shrouds assigned to you see your need and your potential. While you're here, the Architects and Shrouds are your guides."

I blink. "I thought Ethan was my guide." The sarcasm's still there, but it's losing its bite.

She nods. "He is. It's his purpose to help you navigate this experience." She pauses. "The Architects are builders. They create paths, open doors, and illuminate possibilities for your highest good. Their presence is in the invitation you received, in the key you carry, in the doors that open before you. It leads you to what you need to see."

Despite everything, curiosity worms its way through me, and I want to know more. "And The Shrouds?" I ask, now in a slightly softer tone.

Esme's voice drops almost reverently. "The Shrouds are their counterparts. They aren't evil. One wouldn't even describe them as darkness. Perhaps 'shadow' is a better description. They reveal what you fear. What you deny. They summon the apathy within you, strip away illusions, and force you to face the reality of who you are. They do not encourage growth. What you choose once your journey is done is your decision. Yours and yours alone."

Something tightens in my chest. This doesn't feel hypothetical. It feels personal. Like the Shroud saw me, peeled me open, and whispered to parts of me even though I pretended not to notice.

A chill moves through me. Her words sound ridiculous, but then they don't. They settle into a place inside me that already knows they're true. I feel it in my bones, in much the way you recognize something from a dream long forgotten.

"You're making this sound like a horror movie," I mutter. "I'm waiting for Jack Nicholson to burst through the door." Though the joke doesn't land the way I want it to, the venom is gone.

Esme doesn't respond. She simply watches and waits patiently.

"I'm not trying to be rude," I say finally. "But, as I told you when you came in, I didn't sign up for a mystical funhouse."

"I understand, and you don't have to give me an answer, Amelia, but what did the mirrors show you?" The question isn't forceful. It's quiet. It lands like a pebble in still water, rippling memories of what happened in that room through my thoughts. "Your journey is meant to strip away illusions, sometimes painfully, to help you get to the truth of yourself. The things you've been avoiding... they haven't come to harm you. They've come to confront you."

Frustration coils tight in my chest. "But why?" The words spill out, sharper than I intend. "Why can't I just feel at ease here? Why can't I focus on what I am—on the parts of me that work? I didn't come here to be undone. And frankly?" I huff. "Vesper? I could've lived without meeting her."

My fingers twitch toward my pocket before my mind catches up. The weight of the key feels suddenly impossible to ignore, a small, silent accusation pressing against my hip. I pull it out, palm opening around the cool metal. The room seems to narrow, as though the walls lean in just enough to listen.

"Here," I thrust the key toward her before I can stop myself. "Take the key."

It comes out sharper than I intend, the words pushed out on instinct, as if handing it off might slow whatever unraveling has started inside me. But Esme doesn't reach for it. She only watches, steady and unshaken, patient in a way that makes me feel exposed.

A flicker catches my eye. I glance down. The word control—the word that branded me from the moment I arrived—is gone.

"What the..." The rest of the sentence falls apart in my throat. My stomach drops hard enough that for a second, I forget what I was doing, forget to breathe at all. My fingers tighten around the key, not to protect it, but to steady myself.

Esme's brows lift just enough to register concern without crowding me. "Amelia," she says softly, "what is it?"

I look up at her, throat tight, pulse thudding in my ears. "The word on the key," I manage. "It's changed."

Esme's lips curve, not in surprise, but in understanding—a knowing that feels older than the building we're standing in. She says nothing, only waits, which somehow unsettles me more.

I pull the key back toward me, closer to my chest, my gaze glued to it as the new word rises through the metal like something waking.

"It now says…" My voice falters. I swallow, try again. "It now says **TRUTH**."

The word feels too heavy for its size. Too revealing. Too accurate.

Esme's smile deepens, slow and sure. "Good," she murmurs. "The Hotel is speaking to you."

Then her lips tilt with something between sympathy and certainty. "No one asks for The Shrouds, Amelia." Her tone carries a truth that doesn't blink. "No one seeks the shadow that knows them best." We don't know when or how they will appear, but eventually, everyone meets them because no one is perfect. The Shrouds are the whisper of doubt before a decision. The shadow before revelation." Her eyes soften. "You accepted The Hotel's invitation because you were ready, whether you feel ready or not."

I glance at my suitcase, rumpled and thrown together, a symbol of the storm alive in me. But beneath it, something else stirs. Something heavier. Something I haven't dared to name.

"I don't feel ready," I whisper. "There's so much going on in my personal life."

"But you are ready," she says, with a certainty that punches through my doubt. "The Architects see your potential. The Shrouds see your truth."

I swallow hard. My throat tightens. "And what do you see, Esme?"

She studies me, then offers a sweet smile, not soft with politeness, but with certainty. It seems rooted and very real.

"I see a woman stronger than she realizes—in places she hasn't yet learned to trust."

Silence falls between us, rich and heavy, almost like a moment suspended, and held just before a leap. For the first time, I let my guard down and let her words land where they will. And they do. They slip into the spaces I try to hide. The parts of me still trembling. The ones asking questions I haven't admitted out loud.

I meet her gaze. "So, what happens if I stay?"

Her smile deepens. Her eyes never waver. "You'll discover the truth that's waited for you, something beyond your fears and just beyond your shadows. What you've forgotten."

She stands slowly, unhurried like she's moving with time rather than through it. Her gaze is filled with intention and promise. "And you won't have to journey alone."

Esme walks to the door. Just before she exits, she looks over her shoulder, her parting words as soft as a shadow and as heavy as fate.

"The choice, however, is yours to make—and yours to live with."

II

The next morning, I lay in bed staring at the ceiling. The suitcase lay forgotten at the foot of it as I think logically of my next move while trying to pretend the storm has passed.

But it hadn't. It had only gone quiet.

My head is swimming. The truth is, I feel like I've somewhat unraveled and been stitched back together with thread so fine it threatens to come undone with the slightest misstep.

My thoughts splinter, looping back to the mirrors, the sharp, brittle sound of them breaking, like something inside me giving way. The image in the glass wasn't just unfamiliar. It was honest. And I hated it.

This place feels like a sick mix of Hotel California and American Horror Story, if the horror whispered instead of screamed. It's beautiful, but the kind of beautiful that feels too perfect, like a still photo of a storm just before it breaks. It's serene in a way that scrapes against instinct. The story of Architects and Shrouds seems plausible in the eeriest sense, implausibly mythic, and impossibly close. And the worst part? I'm beginning to accept and believe it.

I crawl out of bed and go to stand by the window, arms crossed, watching sunlight fill the sky. The garden below is still; the fountain's trickling water, the only sign of movement. I think of Esme's words.

"Your intuition led you here."

"Intuition" feels like a language I was never taught to speak. I learned early to trust only what I could prove—logic, calculation, control. Yet here I am, standing in a place I can't explain, carrying a key I don't understand, and preparing for something I can't predict. A morning like this should soothe. But it doesn't.

It presses too softly. Lingers too long. The quiet here doesn't comfort—it coils. Like the air before a storm, it hums just beneath the skin. My fingers twitch, restless without cause. My jaw aches, clenched from some unknown bracing I can't seem to stop.

I shift my weight, unsettled. This kind of stillness feels staged, like the hush in a theater before the curtain lifts on something you didn't audition for.

The silence isn't empty. It's charged.

It reminds me of the Chamber—how the air there wasn't still but listening.

This room holds its silence the same way. Once Esme left, I paced, unable to settle, cycling between curling up in bed and standing at the window. I stared out at the mist-wrapped garden below. Then I went back to bed, falling asleep only to wake up and stare into blankness and come up with a more logical explanation for why I'm here and what I experienced. The room is warm, but my skin prickles like there's a draft I can't locate. I keep telling myself it's just my nerves. That the tension winding tighter in my chest is residual stress from whatever that was in the Chamber.

And yet, I can't shake the feeling that something more is coming. The air feels too still. Anticipatory. Like The Hotel is watching, listening, and waiting for me to move. I don't want to admit it, but the

Chamber of Reflection did something. It didn't soothe me. It didn't offer answers. But it made me feel. It made me look. And the image in that shattered mirror hasn't left me since.

Thoughts swirl through my mind. I'm still reluctant. Still bracing. But underneath it all, I have to admit, I'm curious. Cautiously, stupidly curious. Too many horror movies with college friends taught me that wandering into strange places usually doesn't end well. Esme said I wouldn't be harmed, and the peculiar thing is, I believe her. Even though everything in me wants not to.

A long, slow exhale escapes. I shake my head, resigned. I'm already here. And the truth is, I'm not ready to go back to the office—or the woman I was when I was in it. So maybe I'll see where this leads.

A knock at the door rouses me from my thoughts. I turn, smoothing my hands down the sweatshirt I fell asleep in before crossing the room to answer. Once I do, Ethan stands on the other side. He smiles; his posture relaxed. His linen shirt is casually open at the collar, a style that seems to suit him, revealing a trace of dark hair.

There's something about Ethan that unsettles me. It isn't because he's out of place, but because he isn't.

He belongs here in a way that feels intentional, as if The Hotel shaped him from its own silence. He doesn't intrude. He simply is, and somehow, that's more disarming than charm or mystery.

"If you're ready," he says, his voice low, steady, "I'm here to escort you."

I hesitate, my eyes flicking past him to the dim and quiet corridor.

"Escort me where?" I ask, already bracing.

He doesn't flinch. That unreadable calm of his doesn't crack. "I don't know."

The words land strange. Honest. Unhelpful. A little too close to the truth I don't want to face: no one's steering this but me.

I narrow my eyes. "You don't know? You don't have some kind of blueprint for which 'Chambers' are meant for me?"

He doesn't flinch. "Your key will guide you, Amelia. Just like yesterday. You'll know when you're standing in front of the right door."

A pause.

I exhale sharply. "Is it going to be like yesterday?" My voice dips, quiet but tight. "Because if it is, I'm not sure I can do it again. That wasn't enlightening. That was... unnerving."

Ethan's expression doesn't shift, but something in his eyes softens. He nods once, slowly. "It was supposed to be."

I open my mouth to argue, but he beats me to it.

"You weren't harmed. And you won't be." His voice is steady but gentle, like stone worn smooth by time. "But unnerved?" He lifts a shoulder in a quiet shrug. "That means it touched something. That means it mattered." He studies me for a long moment. "Discomfort has a purpose, Amelia. It's what wakes us up when ease has made us numb."

The silence between us stretches.

"You're not the same as you were yesterday and, I'm supposing the new word on your key confirms it," he adds, voice dipping lower. "I can see it already, though, in fairness I'm trained to notice. It's in the way you hesitate. The way you're listening to me now, even when you don't want to." His gaze holds mine. "And your key... is waiting."

I don't answer. But something in me tilts. Not surrender, not yet, but the edge of resistance has softened. I'm still scared. But maybe I'm also so curious I can't help myself.

Ethan steps back, not rushing me, just opening the way, as if he knows I'll follow, even before I do. "You said it was unnerving," he repeats. "But the fact that you're still standing here means you can take it."

12

Same as yesterday, we again walk the softly lit corridor. The doors seem different than yesterday. They are identical in construction, crafted from polished oak, which gleams like deep, aged honey under the glow of the sconces. The wood is flawless at first glance, but the longer I look, the more the grain seems to shift, swirling in patterns that resemble whispering faces and curling vines. As someone in the construction industry, I appreciate the work that has made The Hotel beautiful. The craftsmanship is flawless—too flawless—with the suggestion of movement trapped just beneath the surface, like a pulse caught in wood. I don't think I'm wrong when I say this place is alive. There is a presence here. Each door feels old in the way myths are old—beyond age, beyond erosion. Their surfaces gleam with a luster that doesn't catch the light so much as remember it. I know they've stood here longer than memory allows. And as I pass, I swear they stir. They've inhaled the footsteps of those who came before me, tasted their hesitation, held their secrets.

The brass plates affixed to each one aren't simply different. They're deliberate. They gleam like truths too dangerous to speak aloud—each one distinct, each one aware. Some shine too brightly, as if trying to blind you from what you're not ready to see. Others are dulled, their surfaces bruised and blistered, like they've borne witness to centuries of unraveling. I don't know what's behind them, but I know each door is more than wood and metal.

They're thresholds.

And they are watching me decide. Some shimmer too brightly, reflecting candlelight in warped ribbons that twist your reflection until you're not sure if it's you looking back. Others are dulled and bruised by time, their surfaces mottled with corrosion, like they've tasted too much sorrow. The engravings vary wildly—some echo symbols I half-remember from textbooks or temples, and others seem to recoil if I look too long, as though aware of being seen. One resembles a constellation caught mid-collapse; another, a language that slithers the longer I stare. They're not just markers. They're thresholds with teeth. And I can feel it—each one measuring me as I pass by, as if deciding whether I'm meant to enter... or meant to stay out.

One plate bears the engraving of an open hand. Still, upon closer inspection, the palm's lines are etched with tiny, labyrinthine pathways that seem to shift when glanced at from the corner of the eye.

A door further down has a coiled serpent, its body forming a circle. Yet, as we walk by, the engraving gives the illusion that it is constantly moving, forever devouring its own tail.

Some plates have text written in languages I do not recognize, delicate scripts that pulse with something just beneath the surface, as if the words are stirring. At the same time, another is entirely blank and polished to a reflective finish. When I walk past, my reflection flickers across its surface. It's me but altered. Not quite right.

The further I walk, the heavier my chest feels. It's a strange feeling. Like the dread and excitement mix I felt while waiting in line for my first roller coaster ride. Perhaps it's some leftover anxiety from the day before, which surely wouldn't surprise me. Still, everything within me seems to be on high alert. I even note the slightest temperature shifts. There are things I can't explain and unseen entities stirring behind the doors, their gazes invisibly pressing against the wood like fog upon glass, and they're waiting for me.

A wave of trepidation washes over me, and I freeze. "I can't do this, Ethan."

He studies me. "Can't or won't?"

"Can't. Won't. Both." I trip over my words and then look away.

"I remember that feeling." He sympathizes.

"You?" My expression twists as my brow pinches. "That's hard to believe. You seem so at ease here."

His expression stays even; he doesn't flinch. "I am now, but it wasn't always like that. I almost gave up. I'm glad I didn't."

"Why?" I pry.

"Because I wouldn't have found my peace." He pauses. "In the end, maybe you'll find yours."

Our conversation is interrupted as the key vibrates. I look over Ethan's shoulder at the door closest to us, the one behind him. The brass plate glows in the hush, brighter than the others—as if it recognizes me.

My fingers tighten around the key card, and then a pulse, not my own heartbeat but from the key itself—a steady, undeniable thrum of heat and buzzing in my hand—alerts me that I may have reached my destination.

I look at the door where the sensation in the key is relentless. The wood is the same deep, polished oak as the others, but this door feels denser and heavier, as if something beyond it is pressing outward. The grain shifts as I near, and the swirls in the wood darken at the edges, curling inward like shadows drawn toward a center. The brass plate affixed to the door gleams in the flickering light, smoother than the others—too smooth, almost. The engraving is simple at first: an elongated oval, almond-shaped and unbroken, nothing more than a shallow impression in the metal.

But as I draw closer, the shape stirs.

The oval flexes at its center, a seam forming where there wasn't one before.

A lid.

An opening.

The shape unfurls into an eye.

Not a trick of the candlelight. Not an illusion. The lid slides shut, slow and deliberate, then drifts open again, revealing not a pupil but a layered abyss, an ancient hunger, quiet and unblinking, staring back at me.

My body reacts before my mind can process the impossibility of what I'm seeing. Air catches sharp in my throat, locking tight in my chest. A cold sweat beads at my temples, sudden, but there, seemingly my body's warning. I feel exposed as if something is seeing into me, not just watching, but recognizing something I haven't dared admit.

"Stay with me, Amelia." Ethan encourages.

"I don't know if I can," I confess with a shaky voice.

"Nothing will physically hurt you, but everything about your journey will challenge you. But then, you already know that."

Our eyes meet, and Ethan offers a weak smile. "You don't strike me as the kind of woman who was born to back down from a challenge."

"I'm not." A stubborn edge coils inside of me, and a flicker of pride tightens my spine. My fingers twitch, betraying what I refuse to admit—that I'll be damned if I let fear get in my way. I was never allowed to back down from anything, even as a kid. My mother expertly refined that part of me until she was satisfied, and I was spent. The result is an adult woman who is always on guard, hoping for the best while always in the back of her mind, preparing for the worst.

I walk around Ethan and stare at the brass design. The longer I watch, the more the eye shifts, and the key quivers. If I'm to accept the impossible, this plate belongs at the top. Sometimes, it looks human. Sometimes it doesn't. The iris fractures into rings like age lines on an ancient tree, then coils into tight spirals that narrow and widen as if adjusting its focus; the motion is too fluid, too intent, like it's deciding which part of me to read first as it assesses me from beneath the surface.

Just beneath the eye, the brass stirs.

A ripple.

A tightening.

It's as though the metal itself recognizes the moment I want to look away.

Letters begin carving themselves into the plate, slow and controlled. I thought they were appearing for my benefit, but my gut is telling me it's more for my compliance.

The truth is only hidden from those who refuse to see.

The words settle into the metal, their etching impossibly deep, and somehow, I feel this is more than a message.

It's a diagnosis.

My shoulders tighten as I take them in, the room pressing in like a hush that makes it feel almost sentient. Doors mean something, and this one…it feels like a warning and an invitation.

The air around me holds a tight, listening stillness as I close my fingers around the key, trying, but failing, to steady the rush beneath my ribs.

"Which Chamber is this?" A shudder hits my shoulders as I query Ethan.

"The Chamber of Precision." The title falls from his lips, and he offers no other explanation.

I reach forward with the key, but it feels like the air itself complies, thick with unspoken invitation. The buzzing in my hand provides an anchor to reality as I press it into the lock's carved hollow. The moment it meets the door, a subtle click sounds beneath, and the door awakens, opening in the way something hungry parts its teeth.

I move with a slow, deliberate pace. I'm better prepared today than yesterday for the beckoning beyond the threshold. The darkness inside does not sit empty. It waits like it's a living thing stretched taut across the unseen. The air settles against my skin and curls into the spaces between what I think and what I fear. A creeping chill slides down my spine like bloodless, icy fingers. Somehow, I can feel them gauging my reaction as they trace every vertebrae.

I want to say more, but instinct warns me I shouldn't speak, especially now I know there are entities within this sentient building, and they're listening. Words have weight and are open to interpretation, even by mythical beings. But I can't help myself, and the words come anyway.

"There's some crazy stuff going on in this place," I murmur, but my attempt at levity falls flat. The words dissipate into the silence, absorbed by the shadows.

Nothing echoes back. And still, the door summons me to enter.

Ethan steps beside me, his voice quiet. "I'll be waiting for you after your journey."

I swallow. "And you're sure there isn't anything in there that will prevent me from coming out?"

He shakes his head. "Nothing will touch you, but all will expand your mind."

The door inches wider as the darkness yawns. Something inside me tightens and twists, but it isn't entirely fear. Beneath the instinct to flinch, something else unfurls, a whisper of longing. Recognition. Fear and curiosity make a potent cocktail, and they swirl sharp and heady in my bloodstream.

I step forward, and the eye seals shut, locking me out—or locking something deeper in. The dark swallows me whole while the door behind me drifts closed with a final, knowing hush.

13

They say the mind bends before it breaks. I used to think that was dramatic—until now.

I drag in air as slowly and deliberately as possible, but what fills my lungs isn't just oxygen. It's memory. Recognition slides in like a needle—sharp, clean, and immediate—and anchors cold in my chest.

The effect is visceral. The Chamber of Precision is an exact replica of my home office. It's perfect. Not just in structure, size, shape, and arrangement. It reeks of familiarity. Everything is as it should be—the walls, the desk, the meticulously arranged bookshelves. No, not as it should be. As it is. The sight is unnerving in its accuracy. The chair sits at a leftward tilt, which I prefer. The backrest is angled to the precise degree I constantly adjust it. The small, antique floral dish I found at a street market in Paris rests on my desk, holding three paper clips, one of which is slightly bent from the way I twist it between my fingers when deep in thought. It's a habit. A tell. A precise mark of my existence. And it's here, along with the exact and all too familiar scent that wraps around me. It's so achingly mine. Old books. Ink. A whisper of vanilla. At home, it's a comfort. Here, it sinks in like a memory with teeth, making it into something unholy.

I should find comfort in this replication. Just hours ago, I was ready to go home. But instead, the mimicry clings uncomfortably. My muscles tighten. It's a desecration of my "sacred" space, and I feel violated. I attempt a slow inhale and an even slower exhale, but it doesn't help. This isn't simply a clever illusion. This is mine, lifted from my life and placed here with surgical precision. My body reacts, and I don't like what I'm feeling. The Hotel intruded and, like a thief, stole the place that gives me peace. That angers me.

My pulse hammers hot in my neck and ears. The beat reaches my head with the pressure of rising blood. Still, my face remains unreadable. Practiced and controlled. I would think this a trick, but I'm learning. The Hotel doesn't deal in tricks. It reveals and resurrects. It replicates. And this? This is sick. It's intimate theft. A violation so precise it feels personal. Because it absolutely is.

I look around at more details, and the truth of how deeply it knows me lands like a punch when my gaze catches the metronome. It was a gift from my first—and only—love: Christian. I haven't thought of him in years, but the metronome always sits atop my desk—and it's working.

Small and polished, the wooden frame catches the light. The pendulum slices the silence with a measured, relentless rhythm.

Tick.

A quiet pulse. Measured. Exact.

Tick.

It stops, and I watch in horror as the wood fractures. The relic is equal parts treasured memory and painful recollection. A part of myself I've never shared with the world. A gift from Christian.

He was the boy I met toward the end of high school. We discovered we would be attending the same college. At first, he was my friend. Then, the man who saw me beyond the perfection. Beyond the girl who was a strategist, who always had more than one plan in her head to appease the woman who controlled her. This was never part of the empire I built. It's a piece of the girl I used to be. The one with a voice. The one who sang her heart out with joy—before every tune was turned into a performance. And somehow, The Hotel has unearthed that piece of me and put it on display. Almost issuing a dare for me to remember.

As I stand in the center of my curated world, a memory presses forward with terrible ease. One that occurred on a usual Saturday. When Mother had me cleaning my room.

I sang as I dusted the shelves. Mother overheard and took the opportunity to capitalize. She saw a way to be noticed. By the end of the week, I was enrolled in voice lessons. By the end of the month, I was performing scales in the living room for hours. At first, it was fun. I wanted her to be proud of me, and I loved singing. Singing made me feel free. But Mother taught me freedom has a price and a pressure.

Posture corrections.

The perfect lift of my chin.

The precise pull of my shoulders.

She would push my elbows together behind my back, forcing my chest out and my back stiff.

"Again," she would say. Crisp. Controlled.

"Again."

"Again."

Her expectations burrowed into my bones. This wasn't about love. It wasn't even about me. Mother saw me as a tool she could refine. A talent to be wielded. When my voice coach informed her that I had perfect pitch, I knew what would come next. Mother didn't smile. She didn't hug me. She didn't clap her hands with joy. She grinned. A slow, calculated, satisfied smile. The Cheshire curve of someone who had just learned they owned the perfect accessory. After that, there was no praise for my efforts. Only expectation. Perfect grades. Flawless performance. Dishes done. Bed made. Voice ready. Always prepared to be a showpiece. No matter that I was only a senior in high school who stayed up late studying. She insisted I rehearse to the point of exhaustion. My throat hurt most mornings. But I didn't complain. I wouldn't. My voice had become the only currency Vivienne Daniels valued. She might not have given birth to me, but she raised me with the precision of a sculptor—every word and gesture carved into who I became. She raised me as her project.

The night of my recital, the one she'd been planning for months, had influential people from our community in attendance. The stage. The lights. It was the moment I was supposed to shine, not for me or what I had accomplished, but for her.

I didn't make a scene. I wasn't like her. I didn't throw tantrums. I didn't demand blind obedience. But somehow, I knew I could stop this. That for all the years I'd been refined like steel, I could stop building this platform on which she presented herself as the perfect mother. So, I did.

I simply touched my throat.

Opened my mouth.

And let nothing come out.

Mother froze. I remember her full, blood-red mouth, thick with lipstick, tightening into a thin line. Her eyes narrowed. Her hands curled into fists at her sides, her knuckles white as her long fingernails pressed into her palms until she broke the skin. This room—this Chamber—brings back something I'd rather forget, but what I most remember about that night was the silence between us, drawn out and glinting like a blade ready to cut.

My voice teacher didn't stay silent. "This is your doing," she said. "You've pushed her so hard she likely has vocal nodules. I begged you to let her rest, but you were relentless. You broke a nearly perfect voice. You broke her."

Her tone was seething. Certain. And the satisfaction I gained from my silence was that, for the first time, someone stood between me and my mother. Not for their own advantage. But for me.

I promised myself I would never sing publicly again after that night. It wasn't the performance that broke me; it was the way she tried to use it. My Mother had a talent for taking anything I loved and turning it toward herself, like angling a mirror to catch her own reflection. Singing was something that was mine and made me feel alive in a way nothing else did, but once she took control, it wasn't about me as her daughter. I was a puppet. But my voice teacher saw me—Amelia—as a person and not a product.

So did Christian.

He came from a notable family, and neither he nor I needed or wanted anything from each other that I wasn't willing to give. So, I gave him my voice. I gave it to him when we were alone. Because it was mine to give.

When I publicly gave up my voice, I, too, paid a price. I surrendered the joy it gave me because I locked my talent in a cage. I controlled when the door opened, but it didn't make me happy. That's what I remember about control when I was young. It wraps around the pieces of you that you love until they're no longer free. Eventually, they suffocate under the weight of perfection until you learn how to redirect it to your advantage.

When she wasn't around, I sang for myself. In the car. In the shower. On my way to and from classes. I sang when the house was silent and the world felt far enough away.

And I sang for Christian.

I feel Lysander's presence before I hear his voice.

"Control has served you, Amelia, but it's time to move on." His words land in my chest like a key turning in a locked door. "The emotions you experienced from your mother while you were being raised required you to cover the parts of yourself you enjoyed. You learned to use control to protect yourself. You no longer need to do that. You no longer must bind yourself behind a façade of perfection. You've learned what to look for, but too much control can be cold, and that ice chills the people around you. Once your heart was warm. I believe inside of you, there's still a spark of that flame."

My throat tightens, and a lump of emotion forms. "I can't let go. If I do, people will take advantage of me."

"You know now how to recognize the signs. You can let down your defenses." His voice is steady. Deep. A vibration in the air itself.

Something inside me fractures at his sincerity. Not like glass but more like a chink in my armor. Intellectually, I know perfection and control aren't protection. They're a prison. I don't want to break free, and I'm not sure I would know how.

14

"I know what you're thinking," Vesper taunts. "But these aren't pretenses. They're you. You're simply a person who likes control and strives for perfection? Is that so bad?"

The memory of the sick pleasure born that day in the girl I was curdles in my stomach. It's something I never speak of, admit, or allow myself to savor. It was the first time I won. The victory belonged to me. Not to the CEO. Not to the strategist. Not to the woman of measured words and controlled expressions. To the tender part of me who, that day, discovered her power. The memory was buried deep inside. It was sacred. My first flicker of independence—and The Hotel dug it up.

Of course, it did.

"Amelia, you didn't get to where you are by waiting for things to happen. You made things happen. You're a 'go-getter' and you've already arrived. You've done it," Vesper assures. "You were never meant to be more than you are, Amelia. Your talent is in your control, and it's lived within you. Growing. Blooming. It's blossomed into something beautiful, and now it sits there." Vesper croons.

"Festering," Lysander interjects.

"That's a matter of perspective, dear Lysander. Amelia knows the truth."

Vesper knows my internal struggle. Be what I want to be or what others expect. Perfection and excellence, or satisfaction and joy. I don't ever talk about how I feel, but The Hotel knows.

The first ticking sound startles me. It lands too loud. Not just in the air but under my skin, and I flinch. Not from the sound itself but from what it means.

My mother broke the metronome one night. We were home and all was fine. But then, as always, something set her off. Some minor offense. She flung it at me in a fit of rage.

This Chamber memory is a reckoning. A reminder of the voice I silenced in defiance. The part of me

I locked away, then rerouted. The girl who loved developing an instrument that someone else stole. I relished the control and let it fester and boil until the result was a torturous need to break into a field where women were not seen. To be the best because the world suggested I couldn't, and I did. I showed her. I built Daniels Enterprises into a well-respected company because every building I constructed, down to the smallest detail, was a work of perfection. I channeled that heady rush I felt that day into something admired by my community and now the world. My teacher said I had a perfect voice, so I used it. I screamed into buildings. My grown-up endeavor made me known worldwide, and I didn't have to sing a note. It was for me. Because of me. I did that. That's what perfection got me, and no one can take that away.

"Perfection is a lie," Lysander states.

"But striving for mere excellence means there's always room for improvement." Vesper clucks. "Don't you know that, Lysander?"

"I'm fine exactly as I am," I state. "I don't need either of you for a crisis of conscience."

The Hotel eats my words.

Tick.

A steady rhythm. A pulse in the stillness.

Tick.

The sound shouldn't exist. The metronome's been broken for years. But here, in this place that reanimates what I've buried, it ticks like it never stopped. The sound sinks into my bones. I refuse to let the tricks in this room unnerve me. That piece is something of Christian I hold onto.

I wait for whatever will come next. Yesterday, in The Chamber of Reflection, I learned silence within The Hotel is never simply silence. Here, silence waits. Silence listens. Silence finds the places in me I try to still.

The atmosphere stretches thin, like a pause held too long. It feels like the hush before a whisper, that moment just before something rancid crawls out of the dark.

I jolt as music fills the room.

What is this? Some trick? Music. I'm not afraid. Music isn't my enemy. It's my refuge, my guilty pleasure, and when I sing, it's for me alone. The

Hotel is wrong if it thinks it can challenge me with this part of my life.

A book slips from the shelf, and a thud echoes too closely through the charged air. The sound fractures the silence and radiates like a hairline crack in porcelain. I move to pick the book up to restore order, but before my fingers touch the book, the chair shifts.

I freeze, annoyance prickling, then release a tight exhale that doesn't help nearly as much as I hope. I'm not afraid. Irritated, maybe. My office is always immaculate, and I don't like it when something is out of place. Something that shouldn't be. So, I fix it. Because that's what I do. I fix things.

The metronome falters. A single, offbeat hesitation. A misstep in its perfect rhythm.

My pulse hitches. That piece hasn't worked in years, and the item is more sentimental than anything. That's why I keep it. But The Hotel knows something I can't remember, and its knowledge irritates me.

I remember how it worked, and I reach for it. If The Hotel wants to play games, I'll play along. With fingers steady and movements controlled, I reset it.

Tick. Tick. Tick.

The rhythm falls back into place, and order is restored. I sigh, satisfied.

But The Hotel doesn't stop.

A ballpoint pen shifts, almost imperceptibly, then rolls off the desk. I watch it move, too smooth, too controlled, before it hesitates at the edge. For a second, it seems like it won't fall, and then it does with a faint tap against the floor.

The lamp flickers. A brief pulse of light, weak. Struggling.

It's nothing. A mere coincidence.

The feeling of restoring order and making my space perfect worms its way under my skin like an itch I can't scratch.

Tick. Tick. Tick.

I move before thinking, muscle memory taking over. The pen is back in its place. The lamp adjusted. It's a comfortable ritual. A small reset. Everything is now back in order.

Then, a shift. It's subtle. Control is slipping, and I feel it.

I fix the book.

The chair moves again.

I correct the rhythm of the metronome.

The lamp dims to a whisper of light.

I reset the pen.

A desk drawer slides open.

My pulse kicks hard, fast, and hot. This isn't random. This is a test. A challenge. A taunt. A game I never agreed to play. And it's beginning to irritate me.

"Knock it off. This game is over!" I say into the void, but my words are ineffective. Then, all at once, everything distorts. The walls stretch, and the room bends, distorting and warping like heat-rippled glass. The ceiling tilts. It's all wrong. It's all wrong. It's all wrong!!!

My pulse hammers against my ribs, syncing to the metronome rhythm. No, it's not syncing. It's fighting it. It's offbeat. Out of sync. Wrong. Imperfect.

"Knock it off!" I yell as I move faster and more determinedly. I don't like it when things are out of place. The books, the chairs, the desk, the shifting floor beneath my feet, order is unraveling, and my mind won't stop spinning. My temper is fraying because control is disintegrating.

I would love to ignore this, but I can't stop the escalating tension. I refuse to fail this challenge. Even as my lungs tighten and my hands move frantically, I set, reset, fix, and adjust. I force the office back into its rightful shape over and over, and the metronome continues.

Tick. Tick. Tick.

Tick. Tick. Tick.

Tick. Tick. Tick.

Then, everything changes.

The metronome stops.

The room tilts.

The symmetry collapses.

The walls press in, like, literally press in, suffocating me in the dissonance of things out of place. My lungs seize. My hands lift, pressing against my temples. This isn't real.

Inhale.

Focus.

Find control.

Exhale.

Though I fight the feelings inside, the disorder presses back. The Hotel presses back. A voice cuts through the chaos.

"Imperfection challenges you, Amelia."

I jerk my head up, air catching in my throat as I struggle to take it in. My gaze locks on the shadow against the wall. Unmovable. Unshaken. A presence pressing against my mind, and somehow, I know…

Lysander.

"No kidding! Make this stop." Anger coats my words.

"You chase perfection, and perfection does not exist. What you feel are just feelings. It's not a war." His voice is quiet and heavy, and his words settle over me like iron shackles.

The words sink in, wrapping around my ribs like vines, winding, curling, forcing their way into the spaces I had locked away, and I struggle for air.

"I said enough!" All goes quiet, and I take the moment to catch my breath—but the respite is brief.

Music.

Again.

It's faint at first, barely heard as sound glides through the silence. My pulse tightens as the sound sharpens into something recognizable.

It's my voice. Young, untrained, and painfully precise. I'm singing one of the songs my mother drilled into me, my vocal cords weary as I sing the song over and over. Again and again until it becomes less a melody and more an expectation.

My stomach knots. This recording shouldn't—doesn't—exist, yet here it is, each note flawless, every measure controlled, vibrato controlled to perfection. Just the way Mother demanded.

Sadness hits me, sharp and fleeting. Why couldn't she just love me the way I was? Why did I have to be perfect? Why did I have to exist at all?

The voice shifts, and the change is seamless, but the sound is wrong. It takes a moment for me to register, and when I do, something inside me seizes. The volume rises, and the melody twists. It warps. The notes stretch until they aren't mine anymore, and the hair on the back of my neck rises like from the fully charged air before a storm.

It's her voice. Mother's. The Hotel has twisted my voice into hers. There's no file. No archive. Nothing recorded. But the walls here don't need proof. They remember everything I tried to forget.

I feel sick. My stomach churns. The sound of my mother's screeching tightens around me like a vice. It squeezes the air from my lungs as every note is distorted and void of emotion, clinical and stripped of warmth. The execution is flawed. The rigidity in the tone is suffocating. It's the voice of every correction, every impossible expectation, and every whispered sigh of disapproval.

"Not good enough. Again."

The words crawl through my bones. I know them too well. For a moment, I'm seventeen years old again, standing in front of the piano, shoulders rigid, waiting for her next demand.

What curls in my chest is bitter, acrid, and furious. I've never let myself feel it fully before, and, at this moment, it's all-consuming. When I was young, I suppressed my feelings to gain approval. As I grew older, I didn't want to revisit those scenes, so I packed them away very neatly beneath layers of composure. I refused to let her or anyone else see how much they hurt me. But as her voice curls around me like a specter—one The Hotel conjured—it claws its way through me.

"Please. Make it stop." My mother's voice swallows my own.

"Memories do not die in silence. They wait, patient as shadows. When you bury them, they do not vanish. They multiply in the dark and reshape without your consent."Lysander's voice is as steady as the wind traveling through old stone.

The song doesn't stop. It loops. A taunting echo of everything I was meant to be, shaped to someone else's will and heard in someone else's voice. A voice I never wanted to hear again.

I turn, searching for the door. I need to make this stop. Then I see it, a photograph on the desk. Mother and me. Our smiles match. Posed. Forced. The memory stabs deep, stealing the air in my lungs. Her hand was at my back, poking me to stand straight. Her whispered reminder to smile wide. Nothing was ever enough. She always wanted more. For me to do better. Be better.

Perfection was never for me. It was for her to live through me, to shine through me.

The weight of that truth presses against my ribs as I turn away, but the pieces of myself I buried don't let me go so easily after today. This I know. They'll follow.

"Striving for perfection has cost you, but what have you gained?" Vesper asks.

"Much. Too much. More than I desired. But at what cost? I don't even know anymore."

"Yes, you paid dearly, but not in coin. The money you gained. You live a luxurious life. She did you a favor, pushing you so hard. You became a Masterpiece," she purrs. "Perfection is such a lovely cage, isn't it?"

Crack.

The metronome catches my gaze. Its casing splitting as I watch, the pendulum skewed. It's broken.

That memory of heartbreak—the crippling sorrow—doubles me over. That piece is the only thing I have to remind me of him. His gift during a time in my life that nearly broke me. I can't touch it. If I do, I'll unravel. I want to cry. But crying wasn't—isn't—allowed. Not now. Not then. Not ever.

"Control yourself, Amelia. You know how," Vesper demands.

"Screw you!" I yell.

Control yourself.

That was the mantra Vivienne taught me. The thing that's kept me respected in business—and in my personal life.

I hate it. I hate this. I hate the memory of what she did to me. Still, I can't let it go because I know it's better to bury it. It's all I know.

The silence thickens. The broken metronome glares at me like a wound. I clench my fists. The crack in the wood a too familiar reminder of the pain I've buried.

I turn away, but the photograph once again catches my eye. Mother's face, triumphant. Mine is plastic. A young girl wearing a carefully curated smile. The lie I lived.

"No one ever had all of you, Amelia. You took back control the only way you knew how, by way of command. Your voice was yours to give, and you asserted bravery by hiding what belonged to you." Lysander quietly reminds me.

My voice.

Not the trained one. The real one. The brave one that prompted me to sing in quiet because it was joy. Because it was mine. I shared it out of love, not control.

I haven't let myself think of Christian in years, and what I felt for him hits fresh like a gut punch. He mattered. Too much. And Mother took even him from me.

The light flickers, and the door cracks open. A draft stirs the air.

I reach for the metronome before I can stop myself. My hands tremble. It's broken. Irreplaceable. I can't let go of it. Not because of the wood or the weight or the tick, but because it's the last real thing I have from him. Christian. The only person who ever heard me sing without expectation.

I want to cry, but I won't. I set it down gently. I restore order. The book is back on the shelf. Pen neatly placed in the drawer. I think I'm done when I see it—a smudged fingerprint on the glass over her face. Imperfection.

I lift the frame. My pulse pounds as the stirrings of anxiety bloom. The longer I stare, the more unbearable it becomes. That smile. That lie. My grip tightens. I slam it to the ground, and the glass shatters.

The girl I abandoned yesterday in the Chamber? Her reflection is no longer whole.

I'm broken.

"Poor dear. Things keep breaking, don't they?" Vesper mocks. "Take control. Get a new frame. Mother will never know if you take control. It's what protects you. If you let go, your world will fall apart."

My hands clench. I'm not in the mood to listen to her.

"The metronome cracked," Lysander interjects, his tone more of sorrow than judgment. "The things we grip tightly begin to splinter beneath the pressure. Perfection asks too much of us. Control drains whatever is left. Don't let it destroy what you've built, Amelia. That's what was done to you."

My pulse races, quiet and erratic, and a rising tremor in my chest makes me fear I may hyperventilate.

Vesper whispers. "It might not be a bad thing. Do you even know who you are without it?"

My knees shake, but I offer no answer.

"No. I didn't think so," Vesper coos.

The glass at my feet shifts, and my reflection warps. A shadow moves at the edge of the room.

"Go on," Vesper murmurs. "Fix it. Pick up the pieces. Put yourself back together. That's what you always do. It's what's always worked."

Something inside me breaks.

I hear the door widen behind me, silent but certain. I turn, and Ethan is there, quiet and steady, offering me his hand.

Beyond the Veil
The Weight of Remembering

ELIAS DOES NOT SIGH. He does not pace. He does not intervene. But he watches.

Beyond the Veil, there is no sky, no floor—only distance suspended in substance. Memory lives here, folding itself into drifting colors and currents that bend like thought beneath the surface. It is not darkness but something quieter. More deliberate. A hush so complete it presses gently against the soul. This is the space between Becoming and Remembrance. And here, Elias remains—still, silent, immovable—his gaze fixed not on what is but on what trembles just beneath what appears to be.

Amelia is unraveling.

She does not know it yet. Not fully. But Elias has seen this before—the slow, silent breaking of those who have held themselves together too tightly for too long. It is never theatrical. Never loud. The strongest ones do not fall apart with screams or fury. They fracture in whispers. In the clench of a jaw. In the flutter of fingers searching for symmetry. In the fragile pause mid-step when something sacred, like rhythm or polish or control, begins to slip beyond reach.

The Hotel remembers.

"So fragile beneath the polish," Vesper murmurs, drifting beside Elias with satisfaction curling in her voice like smoke. "Isn't it lovely when the mask no longer fits?"

"She is not fragile," Lysander replies from across the current, his presence slicing like wind through marble halls. "She is shedding the shell that made her small."

Elias offers no reply. He does not correct. He does not affirm. Truth, he knows, is never revealed by force. It is revealed by friction—by pressure between what has been buried and what refuses to remain so. It is shown by memory, and today, The Hotel remembered. The metronome. The voice. The thumbprint on glass. All the quiet hauntings Amelia folded into silence—unspoken, unshared, but never unseen.

"She'll try to hold the pieces," Vesper says, dragging her fingers through the glowing Veil, her touch leaving trails of fading light. "That's the trick of control, isn't it? Even the broken things feel precious."

"She will learn to let them fall," Lysander answers, and there is no doubt in him. "Not everything is meant to be mended."

Elias does not flinch when perfection fractures. He does not recoil at the sound of glass shattering beneath the weight of memory. He remains—rooted in a law older than logic and deeper than grief—

because the moment of breaking is not an end. It is an offering. The gift is never in the shattering. It is in what dares to rise from the wreckage.

Amelia cannot see that. Not yet. Control was never her strength—it was her shelter. And when shelters fall, the sky rushes in.

Elias does not move to stop what must come. He does not comfort. That is not his task. What he offers is presence. Unshakable. Unyielding. A truth that will not retreat.

Now, as silence stirs again in the room where she stands—as her pulse steadies and the air folds inward to listen—he watches once more. And then, as the shift takes hold, he fades.

15

The exhaustion weighing down my bones is nothing compared to the ache blooming in my chest. It isn't just tired muscles or lack of sleep. It's the ache of something unraveling from the inside out—a hollow, slow-burning grief that doesn't cry out but spreads like a bruise beneath the surface. There's a phantom warmth from where my hand met Ethan's. Though he's elsewhere, the kindness of his touch clings like a lifeline thread I didn't know I needed. My skin remembers.

I lie still, staring at the ceiling like it might offer answers—or at least permission to come undone. I barely recall how I got back here. The walk from the Chamber to this bed is blurred, scattered like sand across a polished floor. I remember Ethan walking me back, his presence a quiet tether. I remember the hallway dimming just slightly behind us as if The Hotel exhaled once the ritual was done.

I also remember that the word engraved in the key had changed once again. This time it was **SURRENDER**.

After that... nothing. No memory of crossing the threshold into this room. Just the sense that The Hotel delivered me back, not gently, but with purpose. As if it always intended for me to land here. Exactly here.

My body pulses with the echoes of that Chamber. Surrender is a fitting word for what happened to me inside the Chamber walls. Now, every suppressed emotion is pacing. Stretching after years of confinement. I'd spent so long locking them away, polishing over them with control. But The Hotel didn't knock. It reached in. The ache isn't just emotional—it's physical. The grief presses against my ribs and curls like smoke behind my eyes.

A creak stirs from the far corner.

It's small. Subtle. But deliberate, like the room just shifted its weight to get a better look at me.

Everything appears as I left it. The chairs. The linens. The candlelight. But the space feels... off. Slightly misaligned. It's as if someone recreated it from memory and got most of it right, but not the heartbeat of it. A duplicate with a pulse of its own.

I scan the room. The towels in the bathroom remain neatly folded. A candle glows low. Its flame stutters —not from the wind, but like it's nervous.

Then, my eyes land on the journal.

And everything inside me stills.

It's open.

I know—I know I left it closed. I hadn't touched it since the last entry revealed itself. The pages had been blank. I was sure of it. But now it waits, open wide, with ink shimmering across the page as if guided by a hand I cannot see.

My pulse skips. The creeping unease isn't loud, but it sharpens the air. A memory snakes forward— Mother's voice. Not a word. Not even a sentence. Just the small, clipped inhale she took when she was about to scold me. The weight of her disapproval carried in a single inhalation. I shake it off, but the echo lodges in my bones. That's the thing about trauma—it returns through the senses. Smell. Tone.

Silence. Tonight, I don't want to hear her. Not in my head. Not in this room.

I consider ignoring the journal. But I already know I won't.

Maybe Juliette has left me something, some thread to follow out of this emotional maze. Or maybe it's just a truth sharp enough to cut through what I can't seem to unfeel.

I swing my legs over the side of the bed, slow and stiff, like my limbs belong to someone else. My body aches, but my spirit feels heavier. Each step toward the journal feels like crossing into sacred ground, like I'm not just reaching for paper—but for memory itself. It draws me in with a gravity I can't explain.

The words on the page aren't flat. They gleam. They pulse.

The ink is still wet. But it doesn't smear.

It awakens.

There's no doubt now—The Hotel wants me to read this. And more than that, something within it wants me to keep going. That's the trick of this place. Even now, wrung out and wary, I want to know what comes next. I want to understand the pattern. To finish what I started. I've always been that way. Mother trained me to do so, and life reinforced it. I don't quit. I don't turn away. I don't leave anything half-done.

Even this.

Even here.

Maybe that's how The Hotel keeps people like me. Not through walls or locks—but through unfinished business. Through a whisper of what if. Through the unrelenting ache to stay long enough to understand. To conquer. To win.

I hover above the journal. My hand trembles as I lower it.

I already know—once I read this, I won't come back the same.

And still, I reach.

Juliette Armand, Countess de Lumière

The 10th Day
The Phase of Unraveling
The Time of the Tattered Moon

There is a difference between being refined and being erased. I didn't know that when I was young. I believed that poise was a virtue and silence was a strength. I felt stillness meant discipline, and discipline meant worth. I was praised for how neatly I folded my hands, for biting my tongue, and for never asking for more than I was given. They called it grace. They called it maturity. But they never called it what it truly was— performance. There was a time when I shaped myself to the curve of someone else's pride. I smiled with a mouth that didn't feel like mine. I stood in dresses that never fit the woman I was becoming. I spoke in softened tones and measured words, carefully calculating the acceptable amount of self I could show without disturbing the version of me they preferred.

But the self, when buried, does not die. It waits, sometimes beneath the skin, sometimes behind the smile, and sometimes in a silence so thick it becomes airless. I lived there for a long time, calling the constriction in my chest discipline, never realizing I was suffocating on my own restraint. The world may reward a curated woman, but it cannot love her. Because what is loved must first be known. And to be known, one must be allowed to feel deeply, to raise their voice, to crave more than they are told they deserve. I was not born to be perfect. I was born to be whole. And in the ruins of my composure, I found my voice again. Not the one I was taught to manage and control, but the one that rose from somewhere older than obedience.

I didn't ask permission. I simply opened. I let the mask fall. I let the silence break. I let the order come undone. And in that undoing, I learned that my truth didn't need structure. It only required space.

As I come undone,
-J

16

As I step into the corridor, I see a note attached to my door. The paper is yellowed, the ink slightly smeared, as if it's been handled too many times by hands that weren't mine. Juliette's words still echo inside me.

"As I come undone…"

Scrawled across the page in a crooked, almost singsong style:

If you run, or if you stay,
you can't hide the truth away.
Come out, come out, wherever you are…

A chill lifts the fine hairs on my arms.

Whatever's about to happen doesn't feel watchful or expectant. It feels wrong, almost in a creepy way. The air carries a stillness that simply exists. It seems too quiet, as if something vital has been stripped out.

This can't be good.

I turn searching for Esme or Ethan, but the corridor is empty. There's no one. No guide waiting in the shadows to beckon me forward. No steward to calm my fears. There's only a door. Plain and white. The kind you'd find anywhere, except it's out of place here. It doesn't belong.

What I've experienced at The Hotel so far has trained me on what to expect with its polished wood and ornate brass. This door holds a small wooden plaque. Hand-carved, the letters are uneven, as if drawn by a child. Inside, the grooves are filled with crayons: red, blue, and green. The waxy strokes bleed outside the lines, announcing what lies beyond.

My fingers tighten around the key and that's when I feel a faint tremor along the shank and a quick ripple against my skin. The new word that appeared when I exited The Chamber of Precision is embedded in the key, and I'm beginning to wonder if I shouldn't try and piece them together. What I note so far, and in only three words, is that Control, Truth, and Surrender aren't just tasks or warnings. They're... states. Ways of being. Almost like the key is charting who I am, not where I'm going.

Behind me something quiet shifts, and I turn. It's Ethan, his expression calm and controlled. His presence somehow reassuring, he watches me reckon with the door The Hotel has chosen, and his silence has a kind of knowing.

I swallow hard and turn toward the plain, unsettling door.

"Your path continues." Ethan's voice is barely above a murmur.

I look from him to the door.

The Chamber of Innocence

Something twists low in my gut. It's not fear, exactly. It's more like the sensation of missing a step you were sure was there. I hesitate, searching the corridor for anything. But there's nothing. Even the air feels thinner, as if the building has pulled just slightly out of reach. Like if I called out, the sound would fall flat and never find its way back to me.

The doorknob is cool beneath my fingers, firm and real. I don't remember deciding to move, only that I do. One moment I'm staring, and the next, I'm entering the key into the lock. The door easily swings open.

The smell is the first thing that hits me, and it is instantly recognizable—furniture polish and faint rosewater. My mother's clean house layered with her perfume. This isn't a memory because it's too sharp, too curated. It's another recreation, like my office was in the Chamber of Precision.

Here, the crown molding is exact. The faded runner in the hallway bears the delicate vine pattern I used to trace with my eyes when I wasn't allowed to look my mother in the eye. The antique umbrella stand still holds that useless parasol no one ever used. It stands at attention in the corner. Everything is here down to the smallest lie of perfection.

A sudden jolt clenches my insides. The room narrows and the air flattens into something that feels undeniably wrong. I'm beginning to sense a pattern to these Chambers.

My rubber heels touch the polished wood floor, but they don't squeak. I walk cautiously with the same stiff rhythm as always. It was the same when I lived here. Step lightly. Don't draw attention to yourself. I wasn't allowed to make noise. I wasn't supposed to run.

Or sing.

Or exist.

My body falls into old patterns before my mind catches up as my spine straightens and my hands fold neatly at my waist.

The living room is just as I left it, not as a woman but as the girl I was then. Lace doilies sit on the armrests of stiff-backed couches. They're dressed with ornamental pillows embroidered with needlepoint birds still perched in perfect symmetry, untouched and unloved. No one sat there, and my fingers itch to disturb them, to sink myself into what was always forbidden.

For a flicker of a moment, I smile. Apparently, the streak of defiance Vivienne tried too hard to quell is still alive in me.

My eyes catch on the silver-framed photographs as I pass the fireplace. All are of me. Smiling, pressed, and polished, I'm posed in some kind of uniform. I recognize the postures but not the person. The images are of childhood, performed and preserved under glass.

I turn to the sound of the grandfather clock ticking its slow, self-important rhythm. The sound used to terrify me. Not the ticking or resounding chime, but for what it signaled; marking the passage of my mother's punishments. It was a threat, not with words or yelling, but the minutes that lasted hours, and hours that lasted lifetimes. I was too young to understand then, but I learned quickly: silence can be louder than screams.

A chill crawls over my arms, but not from the temperature. It's something older. Deeper. The muscle memory that lives beneath the skin. I rub my arms, but the ache remains.

One photo captures my attention more than the others as I move around the room. It was always on prominent display in its gilded frame, and one that Mother always praised. I'm ten years old, my hair yanked back in a ponytail so tight that it gave me an involuntary brow lift. I still remember the headache and the smile I was instructed to wear. One that was practiced, not joyful.

My starched dress doesn't have a wrinkle, and my posture is perfect. Mother's hand rests on my shoulder, her fingernails manicured and her hold possessive. I used to think it might have been a touch of affection, but I realized as I grew older that it was a leash made of flesh.

Suddenly, a wave of anxiety sweeps through me, and the hairs on the back of my neck rise as if they remember something I don't. I suck in air, too sharp and fast, and my throat catches on the intake, tight and raw.

My body recognizes the weight of this room before my mind does. Every step forward tugs something I've buried to the surface. The ache behind my knees when she yelled, and the way my jaw instinctively clenched when the house fell too quiet. I bore a constant knot in my stomach that was never about hunger and always about being watched. This was never a home. It never earned that right. It was a house, impeccable, performative, and polished to perfection. Just like me.

There is a rising static in this space. The kind that comes just before a storm breaks open. I haven't touched a thing, yet I feel as if the house is reaching for me. That it isn't just aware of me, but every version of the girl I had to be and every silence I swallowed. Every corrected tone. Every time I folded myself as small as I could just to survive, pressed into the wallpaper like collected flowers, flattened, brittle, and preserved.

My tremor gathers beneath my ribs, caught in the space between caution and disbelief. Even now, even here, I fall into form. Shoulders drawn back. Lips fixed in that polite, neutral line that appeared pleasant and never invited argument or attention. I'm slipping back into the version of myself this house demanded. Someone who didn't slouch, didn't speak too loudly, and—God forbid—one who didn't dare contradict. Silence was the highest form of obedience. I can still feel the sting of correction in the air, the kind that never marked the skin but whipped the spirit.

I turn toward the parlor, and my heart leaps from my chest to my throat.

She's here.

My eyes widen. I know she's not real. She can't be. My mother's been dead for almost a decade, but it seems time means very little here at The Hotel because death still lingers like smoke in a closed room.

The sight of her jolts something deep within. She's seated in her preferred high-backed velvet chair near the hearth. One leg is crossed neatly over the other, a single arm draped with effortless precision along the armrest. She's regal. Exact. Just as she always was. Not a wrinkle softens her expression. Not a line betrays the passing of time. It's as if her obsession with control has preserved her, like glass over a portrait, sealing in the image of herself she crafted and never let crack. Seeing her like this is unnatural. Like The Hotel pulled her from the moment she believed herself most powerful, and pressed pause. A cigarette smolders between two perfectly manicured fingers, Virginia Slims, of course, chosen for their slender elegance. Smoke curls around her like a second perfume. In the other hand, she holds a martini glass, pinching the stem with surgical precision between fingers that never trembled. Three olives. Her red dress is structured, form-fitting, and immaculate. Her lipstick matches the color of her nails and dress to perfection, and the creases in the fabric are so sharp they could slice. Her pearls gleam, resting against her throat.

I take it all in as I steady the quake rippling through me. Everything about this moment is wrong. She's dead. She should be gone. Instead, she's here, exactly as she was.

I see it clearly now, the truth I hadn't dared name as a child. The refinement she carried wasn't strength; it was desperation dressed in discipline. Her life wasn't lived. It was curated. And me? I was a feature in the display. An adopted daughter as a precious ornament. I was never loved. I was leveraged.

Mother's gaze lifts from her drink, and her unblinking eyes settle on me.

"Well, well, well…" Smoke drifts from her lips, slow and deliberate as her stare cuts clean. "I suppose they didn't want you anymore at that company of yours, so they sent you back to me."

Her voice slices something low in my spine—silken in tone, barbed in malcontent. I don't move or speak. She isn't here for reconciliation. She's here for pageantry.

I hover in the doorway, caught between the instinct to flee and the reflex to obey. The scent of gin and smoke wraps around me like an invisible net. My body flinches without permission. I want to scream. I want to bolt.

But I don't.

I stay.

With a practiced tilt of her chin, she raises a brow. "You're being rude. Don't you have something to say to me after all this time? I trained you better than that, Amelia."

Words tumble in my head in a chaotic scramble of instinct and memory. She expects an I love you, a deferent smile, or something conciliatory and sweet, but when my mouth finally opens, the words that slip free surprise even me.

"Hello, Mother—or should I say Vivienne. You haven't changed a bit."

She chuckles, but there's no amusement in the sound, just cold calculation. Her eyes sharpen like a scalpel as she sizes me up and down.

"Neither have you, Amelia—or should I say, daughter."

17

Mother's lips meet the rim of the martini glass with practiced grace before she plucks out the toothpick of olives and bites into one. Her gaze doesn't waver from me. It lingers, cool, clinical, and appraising. She's not engaging me. She's inventorying me. The angle of my shoulders, the line of my mouth, the fabric I chose to wear. She catalogs it all, not out of interest but judgment.

"I don't know what happened to you. You had so much potential," she says, voice syrupy with disdain. Smoke spills from her lips like a smirk. She shifts in the chair, legs crossing again with choreographed elegance.

"You could've done anything with your life, Amelia. But you always stopped just short. A's instead of A-pluses. First chair, not soloist. 'Always almost.' A sad, second-place Sally. That's you."

Her words land like glass chips under the skin. My jaw locks beneath the surface, reflexive, a learned response. She's said some version of this before—enough times that the phrases have grooves worn into my memory. But I don't react. Not visibly. That was part of the training as well. Steady hands. Controlled posture. Stillness was the proof I was worth something.

She leans forward, her voice taking on a mock gentle lilt. "You had talent. You did. But no discipline. You let your emotions get in the way, always feeling, always thinking. That mess you called art? Abstract? Garbage." She waves a dismissive hand like she's batting away a fly. "You were creative in so many areas but never correct. That's why I insisted on lessons. Why your scribbles warranted art class. Why your screechy little violin demanded practice. You almost made it with your voice, but... I gave you structure. I gave you exposure. The Masters, Amelia. You had the chance to learn from brilliance. But noooooo. You tried but failed."

The cigarette burns low in her hand, the ash clinging to the end like it's too disciplined to fall. Her voice softens to a silky tone tinged with something that pretends to be regret.

"You could've been on the stage—the real stage, Amelia. Your work might've hung in galleries if you had tried harder. You could have played with the Philharmonic." She pauses, eyes narrowing. "But let's focus on your voice, shall we?"

My throat tightens. I swallow the lump forming there, even as nausea tugs at my gut.

"Your voice was clear. Pure. But you let that ridiculous stage fright of yours stop you. I offered to help. I told you how to conquer it."

Stage fright. That's her story?

It's almost impressive the way she rewrites the past so effortlessly, rearranging the narrative until she's the devoted mother and I'm the delicate disappointment. She erases herself from the equation of harm entirely. No screaming rehearsals. No biting critiques. No pressure so heavy it left bruises no one could see. Just stage fright. A palatable excuse she can pleasantly sip like her martini.

I don't answer. I just watch. Every movement is theater. Every word, a rehearsed line from a play she's convinced herself is true.

"You never tried hard enough," she says, at last setting the glass down with careful, deliberate grace. "You had every opportunity, and you chose mediocrity."

I let the silence sit between us for a bit, not as a weapon but as a mirror. I rein myself in the only way I know how, slowly filling my lungs and holding it for a beat longer than necessary. I'm calming myself as I claim the space she once tried to take from me. I no longer need to perform. There's no need to soften what's always been sharp between us. I see the shape of things clearly: her affection was transactional, and perfection was the price of admission. The moment I no longer had the posh visibility she desired, I lost my value.

My fingers relax from fists I hadn't realized I'd made. As I take a slow step forward, her eyes track me, unmoved. She is still the queen of a crumbling kingdom, and I'm no longer kneeling. I find my voice. It's quiet but steady, and this time, I'm not waiting for permission to speak.

"You've rewritten the script, I see—and all to suit your purposes, of course. I got A's and not A-pluses because your perfection rules pressed in so tightly that I could barely move inside my own skin. Though I'm sure you conveniently forgot, I gave myself an ulcer from the pressure." My voice doesn't rise, staying calm and steady as truth slices through the space between us.

I step farther into the room. She doesn't flinch and doesn't blink. I meet her eyes anyway, letting her see my intent with every word.

"I didn't pursue my voice because I didn't want to perform for people who would love the song but not my soul." I pause. "I'm sure you're familiar with the concept."

Another step. Each one is heavier than the last.

"I didn't study the Masters in art class because I didn't want to imitate dead men's brushstrokes just to earn your applause. I preferred Impressionists, who looked beautiful from a distance but close up were a hot mess, or the abstract art of Picasso, whose fragmented art imitated my life."

Her jaw tightens. It's subtle, but I see it. It's her only tell and the only indication that she's hearing me.

My tone softens, the words pulling from somewhere deep inside of me that's honest and sore.

"You didn't teach me excellence. You taught me how to disappear inside of it."

Then I turn away from her, but not out of defiance. Not because I feel I've won. But because I'm done. It isn't rebellion. It's release.

Purged of some of the ghosts who've haunted me, I expect The Hotel to react. For the room to shift. For the walls to uncoil, as though they've been listening —and I feel they have—but none of that happens. The silence that follows isn't relief. It's anticipation. The Hotel isn't finished with me yet.

I look down, and on the table beside me is the photograph. The one she always said was her favorite. I press my thumb against the glass, not just over her face but over mine as well. It's a small act. A mutual erasure.

Then something in the corner shifts. I feel it rather than see it, but it seems, somehow, The Hotel has recognized the change.

I wish I felt powerful or victorious, but what I feel is hollow. The truth was a knife I held too long, and now my chest aches. Not with regret but the cost of naming things aloud for the truth of what they were because I didn't escape their pain, but was released.

I broke the spell, but I bled to do it.

18

We stare at each other. The silence stretches between us like something drawn thin and brittle and refusing to break. My mother doesn't speak. She just looks at me with that same unreadable stillness she always wore when she was deciding whether I was worth the effort of her words. That mask of elegant disapproval never needed volume to be loud. But something has shifted. Not in her. She remains exactly as I remember, poised and untouched.

It's the room.

The air thickens around us subtly, as though the house has ears and is listening. The scent of gin and cigarette smoke dulls. A draft curls in from the open doorway, carrying a hush from the hall that feels dense and strange.

Then, a sound.

Soft.

Fabric shifting.

Instinctively, I turn toward it. Beyond it, at the far end of the hallway, a wine-colored velvet curtain hangs heavy—too heavy for this house. It doesn't belong in any memory I have of this place, but it's been waiting all the same.

Slowly, I step toward it. My mother doesn't stop me. She doesn't even glance up. The curtain radiates warmth, not physical heat, but a presence, like something alive waits on the other side.

I reach out and touch the fabric. It's smooth, weighty, and warmer than it should be. I pull it back.

Behind it, where a linen closet should have been, is a small hollow space. In that space, curled into the corner with her knees drawn up to her chest, is a child.

She can't be more than six years old. Pale tights. Scuffed Mary Janes. A checkered-pattern dress with a large white collar, too stiff for playing. Her hair is dark, a tangled curtain around her face. One hand clutches a faded paintbrush, its bristles hardened with long-dried paint. The other rests flat against her chest like she's holding something inside. My whole body freezes.

I know her.

Not from photographs but from the ache that pulses behind my ribs at the sight of her. The silent calculation in her wide eyes... Am I too much? Too loud? Too strange, I've lived that.

She looks up slowly, startled. She never expected anyone to see her. It's almost like she's been waiting here for years, hiding from the world, hoping someone might come to rescue her while never truly believing they would.

There are no tears in her eyes. Just exhaustion. The kind that sinks into your bones when you've been vanishing your whole life.

I drop to my knees.

I don't speak to her at first. I just hold out my hand, open and unthreatening. The girl studies it as if it might disappear if she reaches for it. Then, after a long moment, she leans forward and presses the paintbrush into my palm. Her fingers brush mine, barely, and something inside me unravels.

"I left you here, didn't I?" I whisper. My voice catches in my throat. "I didn't mean to. I thought if I could be everything she wanted, that it would keep you safe."

She doesn't speak, but her breath changes. It's softer. Her eyes dart less, and she seems less guarded.

"Does it help if I tell you that you don't have to be perfect anymore?" I ask. "You never did. You were always good enough—at least, good enough for me."

A low hum stirs beneath the walls, almost imperceptible. Somehow, I know the house is holding its breath at our encounter. The light dims slightly, wrapping the space in quiet tension. I don't move. I stay kneeling beside the girl's side, the paintbrush still warm in my hand, the other arm extended to her, waiting.

Then, my mother's voice cracks through the air like a whip.

"Get back there!"

I turn.

She's standing now, the martini glass forgotten on the table. Her mask is cracking. Her voice isn't calm anymore. It's sharp and frayed. The cigarette between her fingers trembles.

"I said get back behind the curtain," she repeats, not looking at me but at the girl. "You don't belong out here."

The child flinches. I rise slowly, placing myself between the two of them.

"No," I say. "She stays." The comment lands like a stone.

Mother's eyes narrow. "Excuse me?"

"No," I repeat louder. "You don't get to send her away. Not anymore."

My mother steps forward, her composure unraveling with every word. "That girl is too emotional. She feels too much. She cries. She paints nonsense. She sings when no one wants to hear her. It's embarrassing."

"She's me," I say, my voice cracking but firm. "The part of me you tried to silence or parade—depending on which made you look better. You didn't know what to do with her because she made you uncomfortable."

Her lip curls. "You were better without her."

"No, I wasn't. I was obedient without her. I was empty."

The child presses into me, wrapping her arms around the back of my legs like I'm a shield she can finally touch. I plant my feet, and determined roots sink beneath me, keeping me in place.

"She needed love," I say, my eyes fixed on the ghost of the woman who raised me. "Not polish. Not perfection. She needed someone to protect her, not perfect her."

Mother's composure falters, and the cigarette slips from her fingers. It hits the carpet and burns out without a sound.

"I didn't know how else to deal with her," she whispers, almost too quiet to hear. "No one teaches you how to love a child like that. One who cries when you confide in her about the asinine people and expectations of adulthood. She was supposed to be my sounding board, but she didn't just listen; she cried."

"So, you covered her nose and mouth with your hand and threatened her to stop crying instead of holding her and telling her everything would be okay. You wanted her to fix you. You knew what she was. How tenderhearted she was born. So, you used her to wring out all the things that disappointed you and made you angry, and she absorbed it like a sponge." My chest aches as I vomit the words. Saying them aloud doesn't make me feel better. It just makes me sad.

Mother's figure begins to flicker, and the shadows around her swell. Her outline warps—tall, stretched, and then—gone. But the shape she leaves behind doesn't vanish. It grows darker. Sharper. And then, from that shadow, another presence bleeds forward.

The tension, however, remains.

The room shifts. The air turns colder. The corners thicken with an unnatural shadow. It moves with intent.

I step back, instinctively keeping the child behind me. My heart pounds as the light fades further, dimming as if dusk approaches. Then I hear it. A different voice. Low, silken. It spills into the room like ink.

"She's not safe with you either."

It's not coming from any direction. It's coming from every direction. It's the voice of doubt. Of shame. Of everything I've feared about myself.

"You already abandoned her once," it purrs. "What makes you think you won't do it again?"

As I recognize her, she emerges from the deepest shadow and bleeds forward.

Vesper.

I'm getting to know her better. She's not really a woman but a feminine presence cloaked in something that consumes light. Her face is a void, but I know what she looks like. Jealousy. Bitterness. Sarcasm. Resentment. She's all those things wrapped in one and has always been here. In every chamber. In every room. In every whisper of self-hate I uttered to myself and in every quiet moment of shrinking. She's waited for this.

The girl whimpers behind me, and I anchor myself to protect her. My insides tremble. I wasn't brave at this time of my life, but I am now, and though I don't know how to fight Vesper and her ilk, I don't move.

"Don't touch her," I say.

Vesper tilts her head knowingly. "I already have."

Instantly, the child cries out, sharp and sudden, and crumples behind me.

I spin, drop to the floor, and catch her in my arms before her head hits the ground. Her body is cold. Her hands clutch the hem of my shirt, and her eyes go wide with fear.

"She's mine, Amelia," Vesper whispers. "She gave herself up years ago."

I press my lips to the child's temple and hold her tight. "No," I say. "She's mine. I'm taking her back. She deserves better than the lies you tell her."

The room begins to pulse, not with light, but with will. Shadows start to peel away like they've lost their grip. Vesper doesn't rage. She doesn't make a sound. She simply fades like smoke dispersing into stillness. Not defeated. Not destroyed. Simply powerless. Because I chose the child inside of me. My inner girl. I refuse to let any darkness claim her joy. She deserves to laugh and be loved. I won't leave her—or that part of me—behind anymore.

The silence that follows is different. Lighter. The air shifts, not like a gust but like a soft reset. A fresh beginning with night sounds.

A whippoorwill.

Three owls hooting in conversation.

Crickets.

Bullfrogs.

Light returns in moonbeams and fireflies. The atmosphere warms like a hug. The walls soften to an ivory shade that feels warm and forgiving. It doesn't judge. It welcomes. It feels like sweet permission.

Two easels appear side by side. Each with a blank canvas waiting. Small tables sit beneath them, filled with fresh paint, brushes of every shape and size, and jars of clean water. The floor beneath is protected with a drop cloth, soft and wrinkled. I chuckle because I realize the room is already expecting the mess.

When I look down at the girl, her tears have dried. Her chest rises easily now, and her fingers wrap around my wrist and hold tight. I tenderly tuck her hair behind her ear. She takes in the sight of the easels and then looks at me. Together, we walk to the canvases. A small chair appears, and she hesitantly climbs into it. I take a seat beside her, my heart bursting with something close to reverent joy.

"What do you want me to paint?" she asks in a tiny voice, looking up at me after she dips her brush into a soft lavender color.

I smile, not the way I used to, though. Not for polish or performance, but with love. Though the feeling is foreign, it's the most real, complete, and honest interpretation of what's going on inside me, and the freedom washes over me with a heady rush.

"Sweetie, you can paint whatever you want," I say. "No rules. Whatever you come up with, I'm sure I'll love it."

I DON'T REMEMBER LEAVING the easel. Just the hush that followed, like the sacred quiet after stepping out of a confessional, mind stripped bare and stilled by the gravity of what's been spoken. One image lingers, though. A pair of bees—strange, iridescent things with wings like stained glass wrapped in gold. They didn't come from memory. They came from somewhere else. Somewhere I can't name. I didn't question them at the time. I just let them land on the page. But now, I wonder... what part of me knew how to draw them? And why did it feel like they'd been waiting?

The long, quiet opportunity found me later in the garden, seated on a stone bench surrounded by cypress trees that don't whisper so much as they watch. A small leather-bound book waited there, left open to a poem I didn't recognize but somehow knew was meant for me. I read it once. Then twice. The words didn't soothe, but they stayed.

Beside it, a sketch pad and a tin of pencils—aged like they'd been waiting for years, not hours—appeared. I used to sketch. Poorly. Messy lines. Disproportionate eyes. But I loved color; it brought happiness to my otherwise black-and-white life. So I picked up a pencil and let my hand wander—not to be good, but to feel that joy again. I don't remember what I drew. Only that, for a little while, I was quiet without being afraid. And it was healing.

Eventually, the light shifted. The garden dimmed. I wandered back through the winding halls of The Hotel and into my room, unsure how much time had passed. The key shifted against my fingers and, as I suspected, a new word has appeared; **UNBURDEN.**

Relief hits me as I enter my room. What greets me isn't silence but a tray of food. Steam curling from a porcelain cup. Toast. Honey. A small bowl of blueberries that looked like they'd just been plucked from the vine. I hadn't asked for it. But somehow, it was here. Waiting.

The Hotel knew. Before I even knew I needed it.

Then I slept.

Juliette Armand,
Countess de Lumière

The 3rd Day
The Phase of Illumination
The Time of the Lantern Moon

I was given a sewing needle when I was six years old. A dull one, silver and unforgiving. Tapestry, they said, was the art of refinement. A quiet pastime to calm a girl's spirit. To shape her into something useful. Desirable.

I remember the hoop in my lap, too large for my hands. The silks—scarlet, blush, dove gray—all lined up like soldiers awaiting inspection. My mother would sit beside me with a glass of wine, watching each stitch like it was a test of my worth. If the thread pulled wrong or the pattern strayed, she'd tear it out and hand it back to me.

"Again," she'd say.

"A lady's embroidery speaks louder than her voice ever should."

There was no joy in it. Not really. Only the ache of what joy might have been, if the thread had been mine to guide. I didn't want perfection. I wanted release. I wanted to lose myself in the rhythm, to delight in the color and the curve. But instead, I was taught that beauty was currency, and every stitch was an investment in my future value.

It took me years to pick up a brush instead. Even longer to forgive my hands for trembling. But when I did, I let the stitches unravel. I chose paint that bled past its borders, colors that clashed and sang. I stopped measuring each moment by how clean or quiet it was, and I started listening to what pulsed underneath.

Here, beneath the Lantern Moon, I've come undone in the most beautiful of ways.

I paint when I want to. I gather wildflowers

with dirt still clinging to the roots. I sing off-key in the garden. I sketch nonsense and poetry in the margins of my journals. I dance barefoot under moonlight with nothing to prove and no one to impress.

Freedom is not the absence of expectation—it is the presence of joy.

I was never meant to be a polished portrait.

I was always meant to be something living.

And at last, I am.

With clarity,
-J

19

As a chronically sleep-deprived insomniac, having an ache bloom behind my eyelids as I open them is sort of a masochistic pleasure. The soreness is sharp but welcome and is nothing compared to the pounding in my head. I didn't even bother undressing last night—making it two nights in a row. Though my intent was to shower, after reading Juliette's journal, I collapsed into the bed, too drained to do anything but sink into the covers and let the weight of it all press me down. Sleep came quickly, but it didn't come easily. It dragged me under, deep like a riptide. It was the hardest unconscious state. Dark and consuming.

My dreams came in fragments, stitched together by the surreal and the real, tangled memories laced with voices and shadows that still drift and linger. My limbs ache, but it's my mind that refuses to rest. Thoughts coil and twist like smoke that won't dissipate. I turn toward the window. The curtains stir slightly, though the air is still. Something about the movement feels intentional and observant, as if The Hotel is watching and knows even the small, simple pleasure I get when I wake and see my white sheer curtains dancing in a slight breeze. It's eerie how well The Hotel seems to know me.

A soft knock pulls me up. I groan and shuffle to the door. When I open it, Esme stands on the other side, calm as still water.

"Good morning," she greets.

I blink, rubbing my eyes. "You didn't send breakfast."

"You didn't think about breakfast, did you?" she gently chides. I'm sure the minute you think of it, you'll have it.

I open the door wide to let her in, then pad across the room in bare feet. "I wasn't hungry."

She studies me for a moment, glancing toward the hallway like she's expecting or confirming something. "But, when you are—"

My brow lifts. "Yeah, because The Hotel reads my mind, right?"

"Hmm... perhaps not your thoughts," she says, stepping inside, her voice even. "But it senses your state. That kind of knowing is more reliable, don't you think?"

I let out a flat laugh. "Depends on what it decides to do with that knowledge."

She tilts her head, amused. "Toast and tea? Something light. Grounding. Maybe even a little something sweet."

I hesitate, then nod. "Okay. And something for a headache, please."

As Esme settles into the chair near the window, I sit in a chair nearby, tucking a leg beneath me. I watch her, weighing whether I want to give voice to my thoughts and then do.

"Can I be honest with you?" I prod.

"Always," she assures in her ever-present, gentle way.

"The Chamber of Innocence wasn't what I expected."

A slight tilt of her head encourages me to go on.

"I didn't even know it was coming, and when I saw the crayon-lettered sign, I thought I'd go in, figure something out, and come out enlightened. Kind of a Zen moment. However, it left me feeling tired. Completely drained. I recovered in the garden, but this 'journey,' as you call it, is anything but restful. I don't know if I have the energy to keep doing this."

"You're always free to go, Amelia," she says without hesitation.

"And yet... I don't leave. I could. But something in me wants to know what's behind the next door. What happens if I stay. Maybe it's control. Maybe it's pride. But maybe—I just want to know who I am on the other side of this."

"Perhaps," she replies. "Or not. Staying is the harder choice, I think, but it might prove to be the most valuable one."

I hate how much sense her words make. I hate that part of me agrees. I don't want to be transformed. I want to understand. I want to control the ending—not be rewritten by it.

I fall quiet. There's something comforting about Esme's presence, the way she offers her words and lets them land, never demanding a response, just being present. She embodies 'comfort,' and I find myself sinking into the silence between us, not because I'm totally at peace, but because I don't have the strength to keep fighting everything that's been stirred up inside me.

The curtains still move gently, though the window is shut. It's subtle, but I swear they're swaying to the rhythm of my body's tension. As if The Hotel knows I'm close to breaking—and is offering relief only to keep me from running.

"There is a replenishing path." The energy in the room shifts. Her words somehow lighten the air, as if she's about to offer something precious and rare. "It isn't part of your journey, but I'm offering it to you. It's an indulgence." She pauses. "The Goddess Experience. It's ancient and healing. A Roman bath. Massage. Oils. A space to restore rather than reveal."

My brow lifts.

In the old texts, it was called The Remembering. Women would walk into the chamber lost and walk out whole. Not because they discovered something new—but because they came back to themselves. It's older than this place," she says softly. "The Goddess Experience was once reserved for stewards and chosen seers—a ritual of restoration between revelations. Now, it's offered to those who need reminding that softness is strength too. The body often holds what the mind forgets." She pauses. "Sometimes healing begins when we are touched with care."

I'm intrigued. "So... that means no torture chamber rituals today?"

She smiles. "Not today, should you choose, you may enter The Chamber of Reclamation and indulge in The Ritual of Sacred Grace. The Labyrinth awaits tomorrow."

The news lands heavily in my chest.

"The Labyrinth?" I echo.

"An opportunity to move to the next level of yourself. A place your soul has not yet traveled. Three ritual chambers braided together, each one a different strand," she explains. "Each chosen specifically for you. Structured by The Hotel itself. It listens. It knows. And it waits for you."

I swallow hard. "And you don't know what rituals they would be, huh?"

"No," Esme confirms, steady and honest. "Each Chosen's journey is different, and though every guest goes through the Labyrinth, it specifies its movements and purpose, morphing according to each soul. It's part of your truth that you'll discover inside, should you choose to travel its streams."

I sink deeper into myself for a moment, quiet, weighing possibilities I can't quite grasp. After a long pause, I lift my eyes to hers. "I think I'll take you up on that Goddess Experience. Maybe I do need a little indulgence after the past few days. Then I'll think about the Labyrinth."

"Of course. As always, the choice is yours." She moves with that quiet certainty unique to her as she rises, crossing the room without hurry. "But first, nourishment and a remedy."

I didn't notice the tray until she turns and it's in her hands. She must have retrieved it from the credenza near her chair when I was lost in thought. A polished silver service with steam curling lazily from a fine porcelain cup. She sets the tray gently across my lap, the dishes clinking softly just before the scent hits me. Warm, buttery toast and the smell of sweet preserves wrap around me like a memory I didn't know I needed. Something about the warmth feels undeserved. I haven't experienced much ease since being here.

Esme turns, and I think she's about to leave.

"Would you mind staying? I feel like I don't want to be alone this morning, and I'm not sure if anyone's ever told you this, but you have a very comforting presence."

She smiles. "I've been told that a time or two, and thank you. It's part of my purpose. My mission."

"And just what is that purpose?"

"You might think being a steward a simple task, but it is more than just to welcome those who arrive. It is my honor to minister to those who need a sanctuary to rediscover themselves. To steady them when the ground shifts. I hold space for what's been buried and make room for what's ready to rise."

She sits quietly again, this time across from me, and waits, hands folded neatly in her lap, her posture unhurried. The silence between us remains whole, neither awkward nor heavy. Just there.

"Juliette revealed her thoughts in the journal last night."

Surprise lights up her expression and quirks her brow. "Really? What an honor. Her words have always offered comfort, something familiar or true. She relates somehow. To me, she feels like a friend I've known forever, yet have never met."

I mull that thought over as steam rises from my cup. It does seem that way. Juliette had the same concerns as other women, but simply lived at a different time.

"You've never met her?"

"No—or at least, not in the conventional sense. Juliette has shared thoughts with me, just as she has you."

"How do you know she really exists if you've never seen her?"

"I'll ask you that same question when your time here is done."

I nod, then look outside, beyond the window, where a bird sings its song —a sweet, small reminder that the world continues, even when ours pauses between heartbeats.

My fingers wrap around the porcelain cup and I trace the handle. Ornate. Delicate. It looks ceremonial, almost sacred, as if it were meant for this moment. I raise the cup to my lips and indulge in the scent, inhaling the distinctive smell of chamomile, along with something softer, that rouses a memory I can't yet identify.

"I sense you want to say something." Esme's voice is hushed, her tone seemingly softer than the steam curling between us. "Please know you may always speak your mind freely. Whatever you say stays with me. Your confidence is safe."

I don't immediately answer, but she is right in her supposition. There's so much swirling inside me and not enough space between the thoughts to give them a voice. They bounce like a ball in an arcade machine, so I make an effort to slow them and drain half the cup, setting it aside to swallow the headache pills with some water. After I set down the empty glass, I nervously twist the bedsheet to ground me. "This is going to sound crazy."

Esme smiles, the kind that holds no judgment. "That term is surely open to interpretation, but I prefer your honesty over carefully orchestrated explanations."

The words wait, chomping at my lips until I let go and spill them.

"This place is bizarre. It's Beautiful. And Strange. And so overwhelming. The chambers. The rituals. The doors. The way it all seems to know me. Yesterday, I thought I'd lost my mind. And these... what? God-like entities? People who speak in riddles? Rooms that feel like they're watching me..." I look away, my throat tightening. "If I left today... If I told someone about what's happened to me here... all of this... no one would believe me. I wouldn't believe me."

Esme doesn't rush to respond. She lets the comments sit for a few beats. Then, calmly speaks. "I understand. It is a difficult thing to hold in the mind, especially when you've been taught to measure truth by what can be proven or seen."

She looks to the window, her gaze soft. "The Hotel was created for you but is older than belief. Its rituals are as ancient as days and as knowing as time itself. It does not exist to be understood. It exists to transform. Those who are chosen are special. They are the fragments of the universe—us—who have the ability to change the world, whether that audience is small or large. Every Chosen is invited, not dragged into their haven. Everyone who accepts their challenges is changed in one way or another. For some, it feels like madness—until it feels like truth—and truth is neither bad nor good. It simply is a catalyst. Leaving it be can cause it to go stagnant, but if it is given wings, it will fly."

The words settle. I don't know what to believe or disbelieve, and I think that space where it sits in limbo is the most unsettling place to be.

"This has gotten really heavy, so… about that Goddess experience… can you assure me comfort?"

"Oh, yes." She smiles. "The Ritual of Sacred Grace is something you won't soon forget."

I look to the window where the curtains still sway, soft and slow, like a lullaby. I don't know if I'm ready for what comes next.

20

Esme walks beside me in silence. The crisp slapping sound of my flip-flops echoes with the reminder of my casual, ordinary world. We reach a turn in the corridor, and she stops.

"Beyond this point, is only for you." Her words settle in with unexpected gravity, as though they've brushed against something buried inside of me. I glance at her, a little nervous and uncertain, as everything I've experienced so far has been challenging. Still, Esme's warm, comforting smile leads me to believe today's experience will be different.

"Enjoy." She turns, and I watch as the distance between us grows, the sound of her footsteps fading away as she returns to the central part of The Hotel.

I turn and start down a narrow hallway lined with colorful tiles. The light fades gradually the deeper I walk into the quiet corridor. The path is not enveloped in darkness, but the gradual reduction of light melts from bright light into a golden dimness that softens wherever it touches. The air shifts, as I've often experienced here. It's never unpleasant but always something warm and dense, perfumed with a scent that stirs my memories, much like incense evokes recollections from dreams. I remove my flip-flops. There's something grounding in the soft scrape of my bare feet against stone. The sound is subtle, but it echoes inward—each step a quiet permission to shed what doesn't belong here. With every stride, I feel the outside world loosen its grip, sloughing off in fragments I no longer need.

The key subtly vibrates in front of the only door I see. It is carved from deep, warm mahogany, the kind of wood that draws the eye before you realize you're staring. The grain runs in long, fluid currents, almost too deliberate, as though the wood remembers the river it once followed. Soft gold veins catch the light beneath the surface—subtle, not flashy—threads woven into the heart of the door rather than laid on top of it. I pause, fingertips hovering close without touching. It feels alive. Not literally, but in that way certain things do when they're meant for you, humming with a quiet anticipation I can't quite name.

At eye level sits a plaque: a brushed brass panel, aged to a quiet glow, the edges framed with delicate raised filigree. The design is unmistakably Juliette's influence—ornate, feminine, purposeful.

Centered on the plaque is an engraving of a woman rising from a pool of swirling lines. She is not nude or exposed; she is emerging, wrapped in soft arcs that could be interpreted as silk, wind, or water.

I insert the key and enter the room. Ahead of the threshold, a woman waits.

She stands cloaked in white linen, her face partially veiled. She does not move. She does not speak. She simply is—present in a way that feels eternal. Not a figure of authority, nor of judgment, but of quiet knowing. As if she's not meeting me, but recognizing me. Her posture is neither rigid nor submissive. She's simply present and seems to belong to this place in a way I never could.

This is not like the spas at home. She holds no clipboard and asks no questions. There is no check-in, no list, no clock on the wall. Only the sense that I have arrived at the precise moment this encounter was always meant to take place.

As I approach, she bows her head ever so slightly. Her presence is as calm and grounding as moonlight on still water. Instantly, I relax. Any residual tension my body might be holding from yesterday's events is released. Without a word, she extends her hand to me, and I take it.

With a comforting presence, she leads me the remainder of the way. I feel we're going deep into the womb of this building. Where before I walked on stone, now, each step I take is muffled by a long, intricately woven rug that kisses the soles of my feet. I notice its beautiful colors and have a sensory reaction as they wash a wave of joy over me.

As we continue, the walls curve inward, rounded, cocoon-like, and the deeper we go, the more the air fills with heat and scent. Amber, honey, jasmine, and something ancient and mineral drift through the space, rising from the bones of the building itself. At the end of the corridor, a small antechamber awaits. She pauses, then reaches for a folded bundle of silk laid atop a marble bench and unwraps it with care. The robe inside is the color of milk and moonstone, and she gestures for me to disrobe with no pressure and no urgency.

I slowly remove my clothing. I've been to spas before. I know the ritual of luxury. But this feels different. There is no shame in my nakedness, no performative vulnerability. Just me and this woman. As I discard my garments, there's a soft sound of fabric falling to the floor, which adds to the weighted stillness of the air. Once I'm finished, the woman holds the robe open, inviting me to slip into it.

The silk skates over my skin like a sigh. It's cool, not with chill, but with memory—as if silk has always known its purpose in making one feel regal. The fabric clings without constriction. It's so light it feels like a second skin, and the whisper of it moves across my collarbone, the small of my back, and the inside of my wrists. It feels like something I once knew. A softness I didn't realize I missed until it touched me like a forgotten truth. It's almost silly how something seemingly so insignificant makes me feel swathed. Held. Grounded.

She nods, a graceful knowing, then leads me forward, deeper into the chamber. I want to ask her how deep this place goes, but refrain. Not a single word between us is spoken, and yet I feel something sacred has begun.

We step through the final archway. The air is humid and fragrant, curling around me like perfume tracing down the line of my throat. Steam rises in delicate tendrils, catching the low, amber light. The room opens before me, rounded and intimate, carved entirely from pale, veined marble. The floor gleams, slightly damp, and the stone beneath my feet radiates a gentle heat that pulses upward through my soles and into my spine.

I inhale deeply, and for the first time in what feels like years, I let go. I do not want to think. I simply want to be present.

She guides me to the center of the room, where a low marble platform rises from the floor like an altar. A shallow basin carved into its surface shimmers with still water, and the petals of a flower I don't recognize float in slow circles. Cushions edge the corners, seemingly placed with reverence. I step onto the platform. The warmth of the stone kisses my skin. It isn't hot, just warm enough to remind me that I have a body that's full of tension and unmet needs.

As I sit down and tuck my legs to the side, she retrieves a polished copper pitcher. She cradles my chin with her other hand and lifts it until my head tilts back. My eyelids flutter, then close. Moments later, she pours.

Warm water streams in a wide ribbon over my shoulders and then trails down my back. It soaks the silk robe in seconds, clinging and darkening the fabric. I open my eyes into a mere slit. Another pour. This time over my crown. The water slides through my hair, tracing the lines of my jaw and my throat, and then cascades over my chest. The sound of water hitting the floor fills the room, soft and constant like rain falling on the marble. With each pour, something within me unravels. The tension behind my eyes. The tight coil of control lodged in my gut. The invisible armor I've worn for so long I forgot it was there. It's gone. Rinsed away in the quiet. No chanting. No instruction for the ceremony. Just this, the sense that the water knows. That the element itself has been part of the shedding within a thousand stories, and mine is beginning to unfold. It is the first release. The beginning of forgetting—or perhaps the start of remembering.

She finishes with the water, and I open my eyes. From a carved stone bowl beside the basin, she begins to mix a paste, and I watch her hands with quiet curiosity. She moves with the patience of someone who has lived many seasons and learned not to hurry beauty. Her skin is weathered but luminous, lined with stories rather than age, and her long salt-and-pepper hair falls like woven silver down her back. There is power in her stillness, the kind born not of dominance but of knowing. Her eyes are dark, steady, and kind—ancient pools that have seen both suffering and softness and never looked away. The muscles in her forearms flex slightly as she grinds the mixture, slow and steady, each glide purposeful. Nothing in her is rushed. Nothing seeks to impress. She embodies a quiet dignity, the kind that makes you want to sit a little straighter in her presence, not out of fear but out of respect. There is no rush in her touch, only care, as if what she's crafting matters as much as the act itself.

First, she adds wild honey, the color rich and golden, as thick as sunlight trapped in resin. The scent rises instantly, warm, earthy, and sweet, and it tugs something inside me. It smells like comfort, like a memory I almost remember. Then she sprinkles in raw sugar, fine and white, glinting like powdered quartz, and I hear it fall—a delicate sound like sand over glass. When she adds herbs, their sharp, green brightness stings the air and wakes something deep inside me, a pull I haven't felt in years. Lastly, she draws slender vials from the shadows and adds several drops of oil—neroli, I think—because the room fills with the scent of blossoms and bitter citrus. Then bergamot, cleaner, brighter, and something more profound, like wet stone, crushed sage, and cedar softened by time. She stirs it with her fingers, not a spoon, slow and deliberate. The paste thickens, glistening in the amber light, and as the scent reaches me, a slow calm settles through my body.

With a quiet nod, she loosens the robe at my shoulders, guiding the fabric down my arms as though unveiling something consecrated.

From the carved stone bowl, she lifts the golden paste, thick and glistening like sunlight caught in amber, and places a portion into her hands. It shimmers in her palm as she begins at my shoulders. With slow, deliberate circles, she massages the mixture into my skin. The sugar crystals press against my flesh with just enough grit to awaken it, and it does. I can't remember the last time I was touched. Perhaps the last time I went to a spa, but then, how long has that been? Two? Three years? The revelation stings and saddens me, but I sink into the feeling of the honey as it softens the bite, melting it into warmth.

This feels like medicine, though there's nothing clinical about it. Simple indulgence for indulgence's sake. No performance. No glamorous spa with all the modern touches to impress me. This is sacred. A ceremony. A blessing, woman to woman. The presence of a feminine spirit I had forgotten I belonged to. I relish the feel. The woman whose ancient aura calms me touches me in a way that heals. It is neither rushed nor sexual, simply reverent as if she is preparing me for something divine, some supernatural event that has touched women for centuries. This act is not one of vanity but of restoration.

My skin prickles from somewhere deep. A recognition. A memory stirs. Nothing specific, but something older than my thoughts. Back to a time when my body was not a battlefield. Not a project. Not a suit of armor. Just mine.

Despite my best efforts to keep my mind free, recollections pass through my thoughts like cells in an old eight-millimeter movie. I don't remember ever being touched with kindness at all. Mother was not an affectionate woman. She didn't dole out hugs and kisses. Everything with her was a transaction. This is the opposite of that. This is human touch without expectation, without transaction. Genuine. I soak it in like a sponge, and I like its effect. I'd always been able to feel things on a different level than others, but when I tried to explain that to Vivienne, she dismissed it, chastised me, and made me feel as though I were less for having feelings. So, I turned it off.

But this, this has me all in my feels.

The woman's hands glide to my arms, her touch awakening places I hadn't realized had gone numb. Each stroke draws sensation back into skin dulled by years of neglect. My stomach, once braced in quiet resistance, softens beneath her hands. There is a rhythm to her tracing, like a silent offering, each pass imprinting intention into flesh. She continues across my chest, down the length of my thighs, along the curve of my hips. Everywhere the golden paste glides, something releases—something subtle and quiet, yet unmistakable. Something falls away, not just dead skin, but layers of self-neglect, of dismissal, of silence. The kind I've been taught to swallow and normalize.

She begins to softly hum, capturing my attention as the circles continue. The sound is not quite a melody but a vibration. A grounding. A resonance with the ancient ceremony unfolding between us. There are no mirrors here. No commentary. No assessment. Simply acceptance. Only the miracle of skin remembering. Only the scent of honey and earth threading itself through me with each inhale.

I close my eyes and fall into sound and sensation. Beneath the quiet hush of the chamber, she hums, and something stirs. Not pain. Not fear. A new hunger I don't yet know how to name. Not for food. Not even for love. But for presence. There is a home inside myself I've never known how to enter.

21

When the circles have all been drawn, when every inch of my body has been honored, she sets aside the remaining paste and reaches once more for the copper pitcher.

I'm relaxed and remain still, my chest rising in quiet, shallow movements. My skin pleasantly tingles from the ritual. The sweetness... the faint sting... the grounding. It clings to me in scent and sensation. She pours. The water is a bit chilly now, and my skin reacts with a quiet, involuntary shiver. It feels like a rebirth slipping free in liquid threads. As it sweeps across my shoulders, it melts away the golden mixture from my skin. The sugar dissolves like whispered promises, the honey sliding away in glistening trails. Each rinse reveals new softness; my skin is no longer coated but revealed. My starving flesh polished anew.

As the water continues to move over my back, down my arms, and around my sides, I feel the slow return to something primal and sacred. She moves my arms and legs, positioning me with care as she pours water over the curves of my thighs, across my feet, and in between my toes. Each rinse feels like a benediction. It isn't just the feel of everything that's touched my body. It's the offering of everything that's been washed away. I sense the difference—not just on my skin, but in my spirit. It's as if every stream of water whispered, "You are not a machine. You are not a role. You are not what they made of you."

Esme was right. She knew exactly what I needed, and I'm so glad I agreed to do this. The scrub has removed what I layered on over the years, and the rinse washes away what no longer belongs. I feel different. There's no shame in this silence. Only stillness. Only surrender.

The woman rouses me from my introspection as she lightly touches my hand. She presses a cloth to my skin and gently pats it dry. Even this act is gentle and reverent. With every caress, my body feels like something holy. Because it is. The divine feminine.

How often do we, as women, forget who we are?

As the cloth is lifted from my skin, it leaves behind the faint sheen of water and the softness of bare, unguarded flesh. The older woman steps away, and I sit upright, my body still warm from the stone beneath me, my lungs settling into a quiet, steady rhythm. I do not speak. There's no need. The silence holds more than language ever could.

She returns without a word, only a slow, sweeping gesture that invites me to lie back. I obey, surrendering without hesitation. Then, from the shadows, she brings a smaller bowl. It's carved from obsidian, smooth and dark as a moonless sky. Inside, an oil glows golden and radiant, warmed by flame while I rested. Its scent unfurls the moment it touches the air, rich, layered, and old. Jasmine. Sandalwood. A trace of vanilla. It smells like something half-remembered softened by time. Like something holy that's come not to haunt, but to heal. As soft as a lullaby and as decadent and deep as longing, she dips her fingers into the oil and begins at my heart.

Her touch goes deeper than the skin as if the sugar scrub removed any barriers between us. I close my eyes as her palm presses flat against my sternum, just above my beating pulse. She draws a circle again, slow and deliberate, sacred. As before, she moves across my collarbones, down the slope of each shoulder, tracing the path of forgotten touch. The oil feels lovely and sinks in deep. I peek at my arm. There is a subtle shimmer left from the oil that catches the lantern light, making my skin look mythical. No matter how many women have received this rebirthing ceremony, I'm now part of that story. Something old and sacred, not hidden in books protected by temples. Hidden by women like the pause between prayers, and I remember: I am part of a collective of women who have remembered themselves.

She lifts each hand and anoints my palms, wrists, and fingertips—it's as if she's freed every part of me to have a voice and gives permission for each to be heard. I accept the ceremony she administers and let myself go for whatever remains.

As the woman's hands glide, sensation blooms beneath her fingertips. My body is a field waking from frost. Numb places begin to stir, small awakenings in my skin that have gone quiet soften beneath her care. There's a rhythm to her movements now, like she is writing something into me with her hands. Not words, not language, but knowing. She travels across my chest, down the long line of my thighs, along the familiar curve of my hips. Everywhere the golden paste cleaned, rinsed, and removed—the oil seals, and some quieter, long-held ache of buried shame, an ache I hadn't realized was still folded into the edges of me; let's go. Every press of her oil-coated hands says you are not too much; you are enough.

Suddenly, I remember... me.

Tears sting my eyes, but none fall. I remain still, allowing myself to simply be in this worship. Allowing myself to receive. I release myself for the remainder of my time. No thoughts. No actions. I let go like a rag doll, and when the anointing is complete, she gently wraps me in nearly translucent linen.

I feel crisp and clean as I stand. She points me in the direction I entered this chamber, dismissing me with the quiet assurance of someone who knows the path by heart.

I go, the linen trailing behind me, the scent of sacred oil still clinging to my skin as I pass beneath an arched threshold carved with spiraling symbols, seashells, waves, the ancient swirl of tide and time. I don't know where I'm being led, but I trust the path I'm taking.

Though I thought I was being pointed in the direction of my room, I find I'm mistaken. A faint mist drifts from another room, and I see a female waiting at the doorway. This guide, equally as beautiful as the last, leads me inside another room. A cool and clean puff of air drifts over my face as I enter a space with a salt brine made of stone and light. The walls are pale quartz. Tiles are dusted with fine salt that glows like frost. A gentle vapor fills the space, laced with trace minerals and the scent of sea air, clean and renewing. It isn't humid like the former chamber. Here, the air is crisp and cooling. The perfect contrast to the warmth of touch and steam.

This is the exhale without ache. A remembering of the divine feminine within me.

As I step onto the heated salt floor, its warmth beneath my feet feels dry and grounding. Every inhale is deeper than the last, as if the air here is thick with new life. My lungs expand in response, pulling in more feelings of the ancient and unseen that remind me of cliffs and surf and the way wind can strip a person bare. There is mercy in the way the wind rages and the surf roars—each takes a little grief with them. Then again, as before, there are no words. Only stillness. Only being.

As I recline in silence, I allow the salt-rich air to coat my lungs, to settle on my skin, and continue the purification begun by water and oil. The mineral mist kisses the edges of my mouth, the base of my neck, and the backs of my hands, cleansing me. I recline for a while, and then, when the room has done its quiet work, the woman opens another door.

Soft music drifts like silk from an unseen source. Notes from a harp, a deep, grounding drum, the distant hush of wind chimes. The room is lit only by golden sconces and flickering votive candles placed in carved alcoves.

The scent is different here. Lighter. Figs. A hint of citrus. The warmth of vanilla wrapped in something floral and almost imperceptible, like the ghost of a wisteria.

A chaise waits beneath a sheer canopy; its cushions wrapped in the finest linen I've ever touched. They're cool, soft, and fragrant with lavender. Beside the chaise, a tray awaits, holding a bowl of ripe figs glistening with honey. A tall glass of rosewater and pomegranate has dew forming on its surface. A small crystal bowl sits beside it, filled with crushed ice and accompanied by a silver spoon. A soft cloth scented with neroli is rolled for my hands.

I move without instruction as my body accepts the invitation. My limbs, still scented with sacred oils, sink into the cushions as though they've been waiting to hold me. A silk blanket is drawn gently over me, light as a whisper, barely there.

The music continues. The salt still tingles faintly on my lips. My skin glows, but more than that, my spirit feels luminous. I've shed something I didn't know I was carrying. Here, in the quiet glow of sanctuary, surrounded by softness and sweetness and sound, I rest. Not as a woman who has achieved. But as a woman who has remembered, and in the hush of this room, with salt still tingling faintly on my lips and the weight of warmth across my legs, I can admit: I had forgotten what it means to be a woman. Soft. Sacred. Whole.

My mind wanders as I close my eyes and relax. Was this same ritual offered to Juliette? Was she ushered into warmth and water, scrubbed clean by hands that didn't expect anything? Had she sat in silence like this, surrounded by candlelight, figs, and rose-scented air? Or had her version of the journey been harder? Worse yet, lonelier?

I enjoy this time and am thankful for it. Tomorrow, the Labyrinth will call me to walk its shifting paths. For tonight, I will drift in the quiet mercy of remembering I am still made of light. As crazy as this journey has been, I thank The Hotel itself for placing me in the quiet between heartbeats, where my soul can remember itself.

Juliette Armand,
Countess de Lumière

The 15th Day
The Phase of Solace
The Time of the Hearth Moon

There are rituals we speak of and those we do not.

There are chambers with names etched in brass and others formed in silence, born not from tradition but from ache.

This was one of those.

I asked Elias once if I might build something new. A place where reverence and remembrance could meet the modern soul. Where the forgotten needs of the feminine would no longer be ignored. He said nothing at first.

It was Esme who then took my hand, and the wind stirred, fragrant with jasmine and something older. I understood. I was not the one who invented it. I was simply the one who was remembered.

Aeris stood before me then. Not a woman of flesh, but of air, of pulse, of presence. The First Light. The reminder of who we were before the world altered our shape. Before the expectations of our station were carved into our bones and we bowed to the desires of others, forgetting ourselves.

When this chamber took form, I did not name it. It waited quietly for the women who needed reclaiming.

Aeris's presence illuminated what was pushed into the dark recesses of my femininity. She—The Heart of Lysander—emerged barefoot and unleashed. Just as she was created.

It was not her power, but the power of release that unraveled me.

It was not the oils, nor the water, and not even the warmth of the chamber. It was in the realization that before I was Countess and before I was Juliette, I was a woman.

And I was enough.

The world taught me to perfect my silence. I taught myself how to honor my voice.

In gentleness,
~J

22

The world feels slower now. Every step I take echoes faintly down the corridor, not with weight, but with grace. I feel like I'm floating just above the ground, as if the very air beneath me has softened, yielding to my arrival. Even the walls seem less rigid, more like a sigh than a barrier.

The Hotel hums around me, no longer looming but alive, its pulse woven through mine. It waits with me, for me, attuned to the quiet shift I can feel inside my bones. Something in the architecture of this place responds to my becoming. It feels like standing in a cathedral built of memory and possibility. If I lean into what's possible, I can see the grace of this place. It tests me, yes, but it doesn't demand more than I'm able to give at this moment.

Its expectations bend and curve with my pacing, syncing to the rhythm of my unraveling.

I reach into my pocket almost without thinking. The key presses into my palm, warm from my skin, the familiar weight now carrying something else—an expectancy I can't quite name. I open my hand and study it in the low light of the hallway. Another word has surfaced.

REMEMBER

It sits cleanly etched along the shank, quiet but confident, as though it had been waiting for me to notice. My chest lifts once, too sharply, and I steady myself with the doorframe. The word doesn't startle me, not the way the others did. It feels... right. Soft. Almost tender.

As if the Chamber didn't ask me to become someone new, but to reclaim the feminine woman I've been trying to forget in favor of the stiff, corporate one.

I trace the word with my thumb, slow, careful, unsure whether I'm ready for the truth of it yet but knowing it found me anyway.

And, tomorrow, I will face The Labyrinth.

I won't lie to myself. I don't know what the Labyrinth will reveal, but I'm no longer trying to escape The Hotel. Not from the truths it may present or the lessons it might hold. Maybe I'm losing my grip on reality. Perhaps this is all a dream I've conjured in some exhausted corner of my mind, but even if it is, it's mine. And if there are secrets buried so deep within me that I no longer recognize them, then maybe it's time they were unearthed.

Esme waits, leaning casually against the wall. Her posture is relaxed, but her presence carries an air of something ancient, something reverent. She straightens slightly as I approach, and I swear her expression shifts. Softer. Wiser. Like she sees something in me that wasn't there before.

"You look…" she begins, and, like moon shadows over water, her voice trails for a moment. "Transformed."

I laugh, a light, real, and unexpected sound. The sound surprises me but doesn't feel out of place here. "I feel like I've been melted down and poured into a new mold."

Her smile is small, but it cradles knowing. I don't need her to say it. She's seen it before, the moment when someone stops bracing for the fall and chooses instead to let go.

I hesitate at my door, then glance at her. "Will you come in for a moment?"

She follows me inside without a word. The door closes behind us with a soft, decisive click—like the sealing of a spell. The room hasn't changed in form, but something essential has shifted. The air feels different now, as if it too has exhaled with me, carrying the hush of something sacred. It's as though the space has been touched by a hand that knows me deeply—a presence that remembers what I lost when I became too busy to feel. Lavender lingers in the air, braided with something to make delicious layers—baked warmth, almond, sunlit wood, comfort.

On the nightstand, a silver tray waits. A delicate teacup steams beside a small stack of golden biscuits, their tops kissed with something shimmering, dusted in light. I blink. I hadn't noticed them before.

"Did you...?" I begin, glancing toward Esme, but I know it wasn't her.

She shakes her head gently. "It is The Steward of Comfort who prepares meals. In every way, it is you we cater to. While here, we want you to allow yourself to be our guest. You are The Chosen and are most important to us."

"The Steward of Comfort?" I echo, my brow lifting.

"There are many unseen hands. You will not meet them, not as you've met me. They come only when a guest is ready to receive what they didn't know they need. The Hotel listens. I am a Steward who responds for human connection—The 'Esme', if you will, but The Hotel has other Stewards."

What is "The" Esme—isn't it your name?"

"Esme wasn't the first guest," she says quietly. "Juliette holds that place. But the first Esme... she wasn't born at all. She emerged within The Haven itself—the sorrow of the universe given shape. Loneliness, loss, ache... all of it crystallized into a single presence. But even sorrow must have a purpose. When she began tending The Haven, caring for the weary and the broken, the sorrow eased. Purpose became her healing. And because of that, every woman called to this role takes her name —not to mimic her, but to continue what she began. 'Esme' is a mantle, not a person. A reminder that what once was sorrow can become service." She smiles. "It is an honor to take the name 'Esme.'

I reach for the cup as I mull over her explanation. Steam winds into the shape of a staircase before it dissipates and the scent of chamomile and honey brushes against me, soft and warm and round. I take a sip. It fills my mouth with something more than flavor, something rediscovered—like light itself had been poured into the cup. As it makes its way down my throat, it settles deep in my chest, blooming in places I hadn't realized were cold.

"Would you like a biscuit?" I ask, offering one to Esme as I gesture toward the tray.

She offers a small, amused smile. "No. They're meant for you."

Puzzled by her knowing expression and indicative tone, I lift one to my lips, curious. At first bite, the world stills, the flavor halting everything inside me. I savor the deliciousness that's hit my tongue. It's unlike anything I've ever tasted. Subtle, layered, impossibly familiar, and entirely new. The smooth, buttery goodness melts across my tongue with a sweetness that carries memory in its wake, as if it recalls something I might have experienced in another lifetime.

"What is this?" I whisper. "It's sooooo good."

"The biscuits are made with nectar from the Lucemora bloom," Esme explains as I indulge. "It is a flower that blooms only within the confines of The Haven. The nectar is collected by a unique species of bee called 'Mehliora.' Their honey was used to make your treat. The result is unlike any flavor."

"You said 'the haven,' but…" I pause, glancing around. "We're in a hotel."

She studies me with quiet patience. "I know I've mentioned it, but what you might not yet have grasped is that this hotel is your Haven, Amelia. It was born of your longing, your ache, and your needs. The structure that houses you is relevant only in that it meets the desires of your heart. It is the essence of The Hotel that matters; not the structure of the building. What you see around you was shaped by that part inside of you that asked to be safe and healed. You craved it on a subconscious level rather than a spoken one."

I silently take in the explanation, and Esme's words settle into a place inside me I'm certain hasn't been touched in years. A place both tender and startlingly true. This Hotel—this beautiful, bewildering place—is not merely a refuge. It's a reflection. A container. A sacred architecture meant not to shelter me but to show me who I am beneath the noise.

I lift the teacup again, and the warmth flows through me like a quiet understanding, reaching the sharpest parts of me and softening them gently. Whatever awaits in the Labyrinth no longer feels like something to fear. It feels like something calling me inward. A threshold I must cross to get to the better parts of myself, even if I'm not ready or willing to move beyond where I am.

Esme bows her head gently and turns toward the door. "Enjoy your evening. I'll see you tomorrow."

She leaves, and I sit quietly on the edge of the bed. The air is thick with peace. For the first time since arriving, I don't feel like I'm preparing for battle. I feel like I'm coming home to myself.

Tomorrow, the doors to the Labyrinth will open. And when they do, I will step forward, not as the CEO, not as the strategist, not as the woman who measured her worth in tasks and titles. I will walk forward as the woman I am. The woman I've chosen to stop beating up and accept. The woman who is ready to be herself.

I spend the remainder of the day alone in the garden, letting the sweet lavender air soften the edges of my thoughts. I walk the wisteria-covered path barefoot, press my palms to the warmth of sun-soaked stones, and follow the soft hush of the wind weaving through the trees. It sounds like a lullaby written just for me, smooth and low and healing. I don't need to name the peace I find. I just let it settle into me, petal by petal, heartbeat by heartbeat.

I pause beneath the wisteria arch, its purple blooms swaying in the breeze like Grandmère's skirts did in the garden of the cottage. A softness wraps around me, and suddenly, I remember—

Not the cottage itself, but the night Vivienne told the story. A winter gala. The glitter of glass and gowns. Vivienne held court with a martini in one hand, her voice smooth, practiced.

"My grandfather was in the Resistance, you know. Fearless man. Hid Allied pilots in the cellar. The Germans never found him."

There was a collective gasp, as if bravery were contagious through bloodline. A woman near her touched Vivienne's arm in admiration, like the story had been hers to live.

Later that year, in the cottage, I asked Grandmère about it. She was threading a needle near the fire, the scent of lavender hanging in the air.

"You never talk about him," I said.

Her fingers stopped moving. She didn't look up.

"Some stories get stolen when they're turned into trophies."

I hadn't known what she meant. I do now.

I see it in the way this garden holds no need to prove itself. In the way The Hotel stirs quietly for no audience but mine. I feel it in the difference between being displayed and being loved.

Grandmère.

The thought of her warms me. I'll never forget her kindness and what she said to me after a battle of wills with Vivienne: "Une femme courageuse, elle montre pas juste sa force... elle la vit."

A brave woman doesn't just show her strength... she lives it.

I press my hand to my chest and feel something settle there. It's something old and sacred and true. A lineage not of elegance or perfection but of quiet resilience. Maybe that's the part of me I'm finally ready to remember.

Later, when the stars blink awake, I sleep. Where most of my nights at home are restless negotiations with anxiety, this sleep feels less like escape and more like surrender.

I open my eyes to soft light filtering through the curtains. The room is peaceful and still, as if the walls themselves are waiting in quiet suspension for me. My body feels lighter than it has in weeks, with no heaviness or tension, just a sense of rest. Muscles, usually stiff, are warm and pliant, while my mind is clear and quiet. The exhaustion that had wrapped itself around me like a second skin has melted away, replaced with a kind of strength that hums low in my chest.

Thinking about it, I know it's more than a good night's rest. It's the space I've found here, within this strange sanctuary. No ticking clocks. No crowded expectations. No roles to wear like armor. Only the rhythm I've set for myself. For the first time in a long while, I feel at peace with that. I don't need to force anything, not today. I'm not running anymore. I'm just being me.

I sit up slowly, the cool sheets brushing against my skin like the hush before a hymn. For once, the world isn't already knocking. Esme's voice drifts back—three ritual chambers braided together—a line that loops through me like thread through fabric. The Labyrinth waits, but the fear I once held for it has softened. In its place: gravity—not heavy, but holy. The stillness of last night did more than soothe me. It rewrote something. Turned wandering thoughts into stone and laid a foundation where none existed before.

Leaning back, I take a good, long, luxurious stretch, and the peace in my heart and head says what I don't need words for; the woman I am today is one I was meant for. Not the girl trained for perfection. Not control. Just living in the moment.

I slip out of bed, my feet meeting the cool floor for the first time today. The air inside this room carries a crispness that reminds me of first mornings and new beginnings. Like something incredible is going to happen.

I head to the bathroom to wash my face and let the water rinse away what sleep remains. As I pat my face with a plush cloth, I see neither a polished woman nor a perfect one. I see something quieter. Something more real. The tiny flicker in my eyes is not just confidence. It's something more profound. A knowing of myself I reconnected with in The Goddess Experience.

I pull on a pair of dark gray sweats and my favorite tennis shoes, then twist my hair into a loose ponytail for practicality. I have no idea how physically challenging The Labyrinth might be, and imagine something like American Ninja Warriors—which I'm sure will have the day over before it's barely begun because I'm no Ninja Warrior.

When I'm finished getting ready, I pause in front of the mirror again and, for the first time, see someone I recognize. Not the woman the world demanded, but the woman I've rediscovered. That connection with who I am inside, and not the person fulfilling a role, swells my heart. What if I had lost her? Who would I be?

The thought quickens my heart. The Labyrinth feels like something to conquer, but the right to do so feels like something I've earned. A door I'm finally ready to walk through. A part of myself waiting to be met.

A breakfast tray is waiting when I come out of the bathroom. A delicate steam rises from my favorite chamomile tea, and the scent of fresh biscuits carries a soft, golden warmth. I sit calmly and eat slowly, savoring every bite. The familiar tea is grounding. The biscuits once again melt against my tongue, subtly sweet, like sunlight caught in memory.

My mind wanders as I look out the window. The strange goings-on at The Hotel no longer feels like a puzzle to solve. At some point, I stopped needing to understand it. This place moves like a dream, wonderful and unnerving, one that rearranges something inside you. Two nights ago, I might've compared The Hotel to the warped excitement of a funhouse, the kind I avoided as a child, twisted, disorienting, avoid-at-all-costs. Now, I view the distortion in a different light. It doesn't seek to scare. It aims to awaken.

It stretches what you believe to be true and dares you to look away when it shows you the facts.

I didn't ask for this in a literal sense, but my soul cried out for something. Whatever that is, I'm no longer trying to turn away. Whatever is waiting on the other side, I want to see it.

As I take the last bite of biscuit and swallow some tea, there's a knock on the door.

"Come in."

The door opens, and Ethan steps inside. At first, he says nothing. He simply looks at me. There's something in his expression, quiet recognition, maybe even reverence.

"You ready?" he asks, his tone low, steady.

I nod, rising. "I'm ready." I feel no hesitation today, unlike my first days here. No trace of doubt. I feel aligned and certain. The boundaries I've built around me have softened. I don't need to control what's coming. I want to feel it. I want to feel everything. To walk into it all wide awake.

Ethan steps aside to let me pass, and as I move toward him, a quiet thrill rises in my chest, light but powerful. The Labyrinth doesn't feel like a challenge anymore. It feels like a promise.

He falls into step beside me, and we walk down the corridor, our steps unhurried. The silence between us is easy and natural. I'm not searching for words.

I'm grounded in my choice. Something in the air feels charged, as if the walls themselves know what I'm about to do and the determination with which I'm moving to do it.

As Ethan walks beside me, guiding me deeper into the corridor, my insides light up with anticipation, and thoughts tumble into my head like raindrops in a storm. I ask questions of him, too many, really, and too fast. What is the Labyrinth? How many chambers are there? Do I choose them? What happens if I choose wrong? Can I choose wrong?

Ethan smiles, unbothered, and answers every time with the same quiet certainty. "The Labyrinth was made with you in mind."

I'm not sure if that frustrates me or comforts me. Maybe both. But I believe him. I can feel it. The Labyrinth is something that can't be explained. It adapts. It becomes what I need it to be.

My key begins to hum in my hand, its warmth guiding me, now engraved with the word Remember from my time in The Chamber of Reclamation. We stop in front of a door. I know it's the one before I see it because I can almost feel it calling to me.

The Labyrinth door is unlike the others. The wood is deeper and darker, ebony black, streaked with golden veins like memory fossilized in the grain. The brass plaque gleams in the low light, engraved with the image of a sprawling tree, its roots tangled with three flowing rivers. The rivers shimmer faintly, as if alive.

I reach out and trace the lines with my fingertips. They seem familiar. Like they've been waiting for me. Ethan doesn't move. He stays just behind me, his voice soft and steady.

"Some doors don't open because we knock," he says. "They open because we're ready to remember."

"What should I expect?" My question is saturated with caution.

Ethan's expression shifts—not softer, but steadier, the way someone looks when they're weighing the truth before handing it over. "The Labyrinth... it isn't a single room," he says, voice dropping a little. "It's three parts. Three trials." He rubs his thumb along the inside of his palm, a small tell he probably doesn't realize he's showing. "But don't ask me what they are, because I don't know. No one does." His gaze flicks to the towering archway, something tight pulling at the edges of his eyes. "It changes for every guest. Shapes itself around whatever you haven't faced yet." Shapes itself around whatever you've kept locked the longest. It's made to transform you… or break you trying." He pauses, letting that truth settle between us. "Whatever you find inside—"

I turn my head slightly, but he's not looking at me. His eyes are on the plaque, his face quiet. Almost reverent. As if he once stood before a door like this and chose not to open it.

"Whatever you find inside, Amelia," he adds, finally meeting my gaze, "let it find you too."

He steps back. He doesn't need to say anything else. The silence wraps around me like a suspended moment between worlds as I reach for the door.

24

I don't notice the shift at first. The corridor fades, and with it, the weight of The Hotel. In its place, the scent of damp earth and blooming honeysuckle winds around me, thick, golden, familiar in a way I can't name. It's a warmth I haven't touched in years and feels like a hug as it pulls me, a pull so gentle, I don't even realize I'm moving forward.

The air is different here, softer, richer, steeped in something older than memory. The sensory experience reminds me of a summer afternoon that never seems to end. It sinks into my lungs with ease, settling like something I've always known.

A creek winds ahead, its waters tumbling gently over polished stones. It stretches before me, its current barely more than a whisper. The trees arch overhead, their limbs woven in reverent stillness as if bowing to something ancient I can't quite name. A single oak towers above the rest, massive and unmoving, its presence less like a tree and more like a truth. Something eternal. I don't just feel like I've seen this before—I know I have. The sunlight slips through the leaves and spills in golden puddles across the forest floor, illuminating a memory I never meant to recall. This isn't a resemblance. This is recognition. A dream that never ended, only waited for my return. A dream I didn't mean to remember.

I scan the clearing, expecting someone to be waiting. But there's no one. Only the hush of wind through branches and the whisper of water.

Then, where there was only a creek before, a wooden bridge now spans the flow. I blink. It wasn't there before—but it doesn't feel sudden or out of place. The air has been building to this moment, guiding me gently to it. The bridge looks weathered, smooth with time, as if it was always meant to be here. Like it was hidden until I was ready.

The grass is cool beneath my feet. A light appears—not just sunlight, but something else. It threads between the trees in golden filaments, pooling where shadows should be. It doesn't reflect. It radiates. It's intentional and feels alive. I tell myself it's a trick of the eye. But then it moves.

"You used to run without fear here." The leaves stir as a voice rides them.

My body freezes for a second, but my heart leaps. This is familiar. Too familiar.

Something tender and long buried curls around my ribs and hugs me. It's a presence enveloping the air itself. Woven into the branches, the creek, and the soft grass beneath my feet.

I turn, scanning, but there is no figure in sight. Just a low-hanging branch that shifts toward me, almost like a gesture.

"Do you remember?" the voice asks again, and this time, the creek stirs in response.

Ripples distort the surface, and when they settle, I'm not alone. A little girl stands ankle-deep in the water, laughing with her head thrown back. Her hair is wild. Her feet bare. She lifts water in her cupped hands and lets it fall just to watch how the sun catches it. On the bank, with a book in her lap, humming softly, sits Grandmère.

The ache that floods my chest is instant. It cracks something inside me I hadn't realized was still intact. I reach out—not sure if I'm trying to touch my grandmother or the moment itself—but yearning fills my heart as my fingers stretch forward.

The wind shifts, brushing against my palm like a quiet touch of the unseen. I take a step, then another, moving toward the wooden bridge. It waits, just as the light did.

My foot catches something smooth in the grass. A stone. I bend to pick it up, rolling it between my fingers. At first, it's just a stone. Then a word appears, delicate and sure: Remember.

The wind stills. The creek flows on. The air grows heavier, dense with something I can't name. A presence settles around me. I curl my fingers around the stone. The Hotel has done this before—wrapped me in comfort only to unravel me. I won't be fooled so easily.

"Who is here?" My voice carries. Calm. Cautious. I wait for the twist, the shadow, the illusion to shatter. But nothing changes. The trees are still. The water is clear. My grandmother's image remains.

The golden light pulses and stirs through the canopy. Not shadow. The opposite of one. A voice, warm and ancient, threads through the hush like a secret finally ready to be spoken.

"I am Lyra."

The name doesn't startle me. It lands softly, like something I've always known but never had the words for. The trees bend slightly as if in reverence. Her presence is not beside me—it is around me. Woven into the hush, the shimmer, the ache of remembering.

Then, a second light emerges. Not separate, but complementing. It ripples beside hers—deeper, more grounded. A second voice follows.

"I am Solas."

The name lands in my chest like a weight I'd been unconsciously waiting to carry. I don't know how I recognize it, but I do. It isn't an introduction—it's a confirmation. A truth I already knew.

"Architects," I murmur. The word is strange and familiar on my tongue. Hearing it aloud shifts something inside me. Wonder. Or fear.

"No," Solas answers, his voice like sunlight on skin. "We are sensation in movement."

"How?" I ask.

"I am the cadence in thoughts and words," Lyra whispers, her voice drifting like a lullaby lost on a quiet wind.

Something inside me reacts before I can name it—a small, bracing flutter in my chest, as though her tone brushed against a memory I didn't know I still carried.

"I move where sound is born, where silence leans toward its first trembling note." She pauses, and the air between us shifts in a way that feels almost personal. "You do not see me—you sense me. I am the vibration that rises before understanding, the tremor across a string just before it sings. I am clarity shaped not by answer, but by tone."

A resonance blooms through the air around her, soft as breath against glass, then deepening into something orchestral and vast.

"I am the echo folded into quiet," she continues, her voice acquiring the weight of a cathedral's opening chord. "The hidden melody in the soul's deep water. The harmony that slips between memory and revelation. I am the gentle hum that steadies the wounded. And I am the storm-song that shakes loose what refuses to be seen."

The room seems to pulse—warm, then fierce, then reverent.

"I am the lullaby that calms trembling hands," Lyra says, her tone brightening with warmth, "and I am the thunder-laced crescendo that cracks the shell you've outgrown. When the path forces you inward —when doubt tightens, when fear cages, when your heart turns against itself—I am the music inside the breaking. The chord that refuses silence. The note that carries you forward."

Her final words linger like the last vibration of an organ in an empty hall.

"I am the motion beneath stillness," Solis says, his voice low and steady, like sunlight trying to decide where to land. The sound drifts through the room with a warmth I almost talk myself out of noticing. It moves along my skin before I'm ready for it, and I catch myself leaning in—not a lot, just enough to feel ridiculous for pretending I didn't.

Something shifts inside me, a tiny flutter at the edge of awareness I can't quite explain.

"I move in the quiet places where fear loosens its grip. Where the body remembers how to open. Where the spirit stirs long before choice is made."

A subtle change rolls through the space around him. Not noise or light. It feels more like a ripple in the air that brushes across my arm in the softness of early morning warmth.

"I am the ember beneath your composure," he goes on, his voice taking on a weight that feels far older than he looks. "The warmth in your hollow spaces. "The nudge that sends you forward when everything in you wants to turn back."

His words don't hit like normal speech; they slip through the space in soft waves, brushing against me in a way I register before I'm ready to admit it. I can feel it more than make sense of it, which is unsettling.

"I am the movement in memory. The quiet rise of courage when you feel fear. The steadying that burns inside and reminds you you're still alive."

There's a pulse to him, subtle at first, then unmistakable—like heat blooming under a frozen pond.

"I am the hush before transformation," Solis says, his voice carrying a kind of quiet authority that makes me straighten without meaning to. Something inside me reacts—nothing dramatic, just a slight tightening, like I'm bracing for something I can't name. "The shift inside your bones when you are ready to change, even if you do not believe you are."

The words land strangely, almost too close, as though he's reached into a place I didn't give him permission to see.

"When the path asks you to unravel," he continues, "when the world you built no longer holds, I am the warmth that keeps you from turning to stone."

There's a beat where I don't move, caught between wanting to understand him and wanting to pretend I already do. Something faint, almost reluctant, settles through me—an easing I didn't expect, like the body deciding on its own that it doesn't have to fight everything at once.

His words settle into me, slow and sure, like a flame learning its own strength.

"I am not a guardian made of form. I am the fire beneath your becoming." He announces.

"And, I am not a guide made of flesh. I am the song beneath your becoming," Lyra adds. There's a pause. "You expected pain."

Lyra's last statement hits me and I exhale, slow and deliberate. "I've not known The Hotel one hundred percent for its kindness."

Solas's light holds steady. "Not all who watch over you wish to see you suffer."

The words land in my ribs, reverberating deeper than I expect. For days, The Hotel has stripped me raw. But this moment isn't about breaking me. It's about bearing witness. Being seen. Being held.

I turn to the bridge. The one that wasn't here before but feels like it's always been. A threshold. A choice. A quiet space between one version of me and the next.

"What is it you want from me?" I ask.

Neither Lyra nor Solas answer. They don't need to. The light stretches toward the bridge, inviting. The water beneath flows smoothly and peacefully.

I clench the stone marked Remember. The choice is mine.

25

The pass through the waterfall doesn't soak me. Instead, I step into silence so exact, so absolute, it feels curated and most intentional. Behind me, the sound disappears completely. No splash. No ripple. Not even the whisper of parting water. The portal seals itself behind me, and where liquid once shimmered, there is only a wall. Smooth and impenetrable, I see no seam of a doorway and no sign that anything ever flowed through. There's no way out.

Ahead, a corridor stretches forward, bathed in golden light that hovers somewhere between dawn and nostalgia. The floors are oak and are soft beneath my bare feet, warm in a way that suggests memory more than heat. The glow touches the walls too evenly, diffused as though time has been paused at its mid-point, holding everything in place.

A scent curls through the air—sugar and buttercream—but also something synthetic. Plastic. Balloons. Candle smoke. The layer beneath that, though slight, is the sterile tang of latex and someone else's lingering air. Somewhere in the distance, beneath the sweetness and silence, there is a hush—a distant rhythm of water falling. It is not immediate or alarming. More like a memory brushing the edge of consciousness.

A doorway opens to my left. The frame is too broad, and the wood is carved in miniature roses. The detail is excessive. Loving or obsessive. I can't decide which. When I step through, I arrive at a birthday party.

The scene is so surreal, a cinching sensation tightens in my chest. Memory engages with something distant I've pushed away. As bits and pieces of clarity seep in, I feel as if my lungs have forgotten their purpose.

The room is too perfect. A scene of engineered joy. Every streamer hovers above like it's afraid to droop. The air smells of confection, but it's overpowering. The sweetness clings to my tongue, layered with the taste of something false, coated in that saccharine cheer that masks the truth that something spoiled lies beneath.

The table stretches long and narrow, its white cloth ironed into sharp, crisp edges. Each place setting is identical, with delicate china patterned in pale pink, forks angled just so, and napkins folded into exact triangles.

At the head of the table sits a little girl. My heart squeezes as I instantly recognize her. She's outfitted in shades of my memory—a rose-colored dress with lace trim, ribbons that never fray in her hair, shoes that never scuff. She's not a child. She's an expectation carved into flesh. The kind of girl praised for poise, not play. Her expression is too calm. It isn't simply composed; it's correct.

She doesn't fidget. She doesn't smile. Her back is ramrod straight. Her hands are folded in her lap, and her blue eyes—they meet mine. A chill glides across the back of my neck as our eyes lock, and I stare into an azure mirror. Beside her sits the blue-lit figure.

"Who are you?" I ask aloud.

It startles then answers telepathically.

"I am The Eye Between The Worlds."

The observer emits a low glow like twilight pressed into form. Its faceless head turns toward me along with the girl.

I'm unnerved. Though I want to run, I know I'm not meant to. The portal would have let me go back through if I had.

"We've been waiting for you," the girl announces. "Won't you take your seat?"

Her voice is pleasant. Too pleasant. Porcelain-polished. Polite. Practiced. A tone made not to invite but to demand softly in a way no one would dare refuse.

My eyes flick to the table. Twelve chairs. Eleven are filled. I hadn't noticed their number until now. Even more unsettling is that all the other girls are me—but different versions of me. They are dressed in eras I remember. Some older, some younger. Each one perfectly arranged like dolls in a still life. Their postures are upright and correct, and their smiles are identical. They sit beautifully with hair brushed smooth and fingernails neatly manicured. Each one a role I played: The Honor Student. The

Overachiever. The Dutiful Daughter. The Girl Who Never Cried.

The twelfth chair is marked with a name card: Amelia, Age Thirty-Eight.

Me. Now.

My knees weaken.

"You're late," the child adds sweetly. "She doesn't like it when we're late."

I glance at the heart-shaped cake as I take my seat and look closely at it. White icing with pale pink rosettes and words written in delicate script: *Happy Birthday.*

The candles are unlit, but the wax is melting. No flame, and yet the evidence of heat. There's a shadow behind each of the girls, which slowly darkens. Then, as if on cue, the candles flare by themselves. All of them at once.

"Happy birthday to you. Happy birthday to you. Happy birthday, dear Mother. Happy birthday to you."

Mother. Of course. We shared a birth date and so shared celebrations.

The voices blend, but not in harmony—in precision. The song is hollow and mechanical. Words rehearsed until no joy remained. I remember this. I remember when mouths formed the words, but not hearts.

The youngest version of me—the one missing her two front teeth—tilts her head and stares at me wide-eyed. But there's no spark of childhood in her expression. Just the hollow awareness of a doll that records.

The candles flare higher, and all the girls blow them out, a single shared exhale.

A girl at the head of the table lifts a knife that's too large for her hand. It's not a serving knife. It's a meat cleaver. Industrial. Heavy. But the girl's hand doesn't tremble, and her expression shows no trace of strain.

The Witness drifts forward just enough to remind me he's watching. It turns to me. The voice is inaudible through the air but arrives within me.

"I am the witness of those things your memory tried to erase." The words freeze in my marrow. "Every time you swallowed your truth… every time you smiled instead of screamed… every time you made yourself pleasing instead of real—I watched and noted."

My attention is captured by the light catching the blade as the girl presses the knife into the cake. It resists. I expect velvet. I find iron.

A thick, dark line appears. It's not edible. It smells of iron and old grief.

Each of the girls takes a turn with the knife. Each makes a slice.

Then it's my turn.

I rise slowly. The blade in my hand feels colder than it should. I sink the knife into the cake while all the girls watch. None blink. When I pull it back, the red line begins to run.

"What's happening?" I whisper.

"You put another scar on Mother's heart," they say in unison, and then stab at the cake with their forks. The child at the head of the table holds hers high. At the end of the tines is exactly what I feared: a piece of a heart.

A sob rises, thick and strangled, as the Witness speaks again. "You are not here to be spared the truth, Amelia. You are here to remember the child who paid for your survival, and to realize she was not of your making."

My legs tremble, but I don't sit. The chair waits behind me, its name card still in place.

Amelia, Age Thirty-Eight.

I remain standing.

The chair bears my name, but I am no longer the girl who answers to it.

26

My skin crawls, but I cannot move.

The girls turn toward me. Not in sync, not like dolls, but slowly. One by one, they shift in their chairs. Their necks swivel with unnatural grace until every gaze is upon me. Their smiles are gone, but what I see in their expressions is worse.

Grief.

Their eyes hold it without blinking. They look unbearably sad. As if I have died, and they are the only ones who remember. Not what I became, but the childhood I gave up.

The realization roots itself inside me like something that's always been true, just never named. The etched place card no longer marks a seat but marks a death. That is why my name is no longer printed but carved in stone. This scene is a memorial dressed as a party. A gravestone nestled in icing. Now, I feel things I didn't allow myself to feel, and I, too, mourn me.

Suddenly, the air doesn't move, but the atmosphere shifts. Not with a breeze or even just a sound, but a tightening like the room itself is bracing for something unseen—and then, the scent changes.

The sweet scent of sugar curdles. The frosting smell that once coated the air with nostalgia sours at the edges, turning heavy, sticky, and wrong. Beneath it rises something metallic. The scent of old pennies and damp soil. Rot blooming beneath the sugar. The perfume of something that was once alive but lingered too long.

The room doesn't shift so much as it exhales, giving way to something older than memory, something that's waited beneath the surface for years.

The wallpaper begins to peel.

The sound is delicate, like paper tearing underwater. Soft but wet. Thick. Each strip peels like skin, like a mask that's been fused too long to the body underneath. And what lies beneath is not rot. It's worse. It begins to peel, not in pieces, but in deliberate spirals. Long, curling strips lift from the walls like something exhaling after centuries of restraint. They do not flake. They unfurl. Each release carries more than glue and paint—it unveils memory. The paper comes away like skin, like a mask worn so long it has fused with the flesh beneath.

Everything had been arranged to look untouched. The walls weren't meant to protect—they were meant to stage. Like a set dressing meant to convince the audience there was nothing evil in the basement. No monster waiting to attack. It was worse; an imitation of life. I can feel it now in my bones: this isn't my collapse. It's my confession.

The truth lands in me like a revelation that's been waiting for language. Everything required of me—every perfect dress, every camera-ready smile—was designed. The house was never home. It was theater. The birthday party, a tableau. The sweetness is staged. Even the streamers were aligned with surgical precision, symmetry masquerading as love and weaponized as a means of control. The ugliness of truth had been painted over with pleasantries, and now the walls bleed.

Beneath the peeled layers, frames emerge. Dozens of them lined in unnerving precision like a gallery of ghosts. Each one displays a version of the girls—of me. Same posture. Same lace collars. Same poise that once passed for pride. Except now, their faces have begun to change. Their features smooth away. Eyes vanish. Mouths blur. Skin-colored ovals replace expression until only a museum of silence remains. A childhood museum curated in mourning. The walls have begun to remember.

This is not the erosion of time. This is a revelation. I've heard people say, "If walls could talk," and now I know what that means. The walls in my home were never passive. They were styled, designed, and curated.

Just like me.

I should look away. But there's nowhere else to look. The walls remember better than I do.

Then I see her, the version of me from the birthday with the scratchy lace collar. My smile is too broad. My hands, too, still. The memory of the room is filled with family and frosting and tension so thick it clings to my scalp like hairspray. Even then, my voice had begun to vanish. These frames are not portraits. They were warnings. A record of the childhood I sacrificed for this polished veneer I now wear.

Slowly, the images flicker. The scenes begin to move. A dining table with sharp corners and no warmth. A woman sits at the head, her spine rigid, her face obscured by shadow, yet her judgment is visible in her posture alone. The girl across from her—me—does not speak. Her fear is quiet, not theatrical. The kind of fear that learns early that questions carry consequences, especially when the answers are given through gritted teeth. She folds herself inward, memorizing the difference between tone and threat. Somewhere behind the walls, a clock begins to tick.

I step toward a mirror. I don't mean to, but it pulls at something inside of me that's older than my will. My fingers hover above the glass, and then suddenly, her voice cracks through the stillness, clear and cold, slicing through me.

"Sit up straight."

Tick.

"Stop fidgeting."

Tick.

"You're too sensitive."

Tick.

"Stop crying. You'll embarrass yourself."

Tick.

My body falls into the clock's rhythm against my will. Inhale. *Tick.* Exhale. *Tick.*

My body braces for the next command as the clock stutters, skips, and then halts.

In the silence, I brace for punishment.

The girl with me doesn't cry. She doesn't flinch. She just endures. The blue-lit figure remains beside her, unmoving. It doesn't shield her, and it doesn't soothe. It simply stays, witnessing what was never meant to be seen.

The mirrors multiply as more wallpaper uncoils, long curling strips falling like discarded masks, revealing row after row of reflections. Memory after memory. In each one, I see her again. Me. Young. Controlled. Diminished. Perfect.

Empty.

Though my knees falter, the house will not release me. It's been decided. I am not permitted to leave until I've seen it all. Until I've named what I became. Until I've looked each version of myself in the face and acknowledged that none of them were whole.

The shadow in the hallway glides forward. It does not stomp or screech like a haunting. It glides and oozes, thick and slow, like spilled ink and regret too old to dry. It enters rooms not with noise but with knowing and whispers truths I've always feared: You were never meant to escape this. This life is what made you who you are.

The girl tightens her grip on my hand. Her petite frame coils inward. Her shoulders lift, and her jaw clenches just before her body locks into silence. I remember these moments exactly. They are the silence that settles just before surrender. When you stop presenting your case by trying to be understood. The times you stop talking because being quiet is the only currency you can afford.

I hold her in both arms. Her body is rigid at first, then folds against me like a letter that has never been mailed. As I hold her close, she lifts her gaze, and our eyes meet. That's when I feel it, raw and pulsing. The revisitation of desperate hope that maybe—just maybe—this time, she'll be enough.

That, if she's done everything perfectly, she'll matter.

"Maybe she'll love us this time," she whispers. "Maybe we'll be worthy."

The ticking slows. Slows again. Then stills. Silence descends, thick and absolute. Both she and I hold the silence we were never permitted to break. A single moment of suspension before the crash.

"Did we do good, Momma?" she asks, voice trembling like the wick of a candle before it's blown out. "Did you like your party? Did you have fun? Was it pretty enough?"

A silence falls. Judgment waiting to be named.

From the dark, the voice I recognize all too well arrives.

"I never wanted the party. Come to think of it, I never wanted you."

The girl shatters.

I shatter, too.

My heart breaks for her as her body folds into my chest, her small hands flying to her ears as a strangled cry escapes. The sound is almost too tiny to carry such ruin of a spirit, yet it does. It pierces the room like glass exploding inward. The sob is not one to garner attention. It's the sound grief makes when it's been waiting years to exist.

I hold her tight, knowing that I'm clutching the child I used to be and knowing that I cannot heal her heart. If I could, I would stop her pain.

I hold her as, together, we stagger toward the mirror. The reflection that meets us is familiar and haunting. It's my face, sleek, polished, and hungry for approval. The year I launched the company. The year I took control of my future and birthed Daniels Enterprises. The year I created something for myself and performed successfully.

Tears track silently down my cheeks as the world holds still.

All my life, I polished myself into something she could love. And in doing so, I abandoned the one who needed love the most.

27

Tears track silently down my cheeks as the world holds still. Then the glass fogs, the light fractures, and the child in my arms becomes weightless. She dissolves—absorbed, not gone—folded into the marrow of who I am now. The mirror ripples, buckling inward like a moment stretched too thin, and when I blink, the world reshapes.

I am in the center of an auditorium.

Not a memory—this is a moment. One stitched from presence, not past. The very space where I had once been prepared to perform. I go still as a melody floats through the room, spectral and warped, like a lullaby played underwater. I know it. A haunting variation of the song I was meant to sing the night I chose silence instead—and by doing so, dismantled my mother's designs, not with rebellion, but with absence. I had refused the note. Refused her stage. And in doing so, I carved a sliver of space for myself.

Now, that space awakens.

The atmosphere feels swollen with expectation. The room inhales me. The scent of dry wood mingles with something floral and sharp. Mother's perfume. It slinks across the space, not like scent, but like memory searching for a place to settle. The acoustics here are cruel—every sound, every heartbeat, every thought amplified like a confession.

Then I hear something that reminds me of... bamboo. Like wind chimes, wooden and hollow. When I glance up, I see them.

Marionettes. Dozens of them. Suspended above in neat rows.

Their wooden bodies sway with unnatural grace as though stirred by a phantom current, not string. As I step backward, my gaze sharpens, and tightness clamps around my throat. Each one is me.

They are carved in a precise replication of me—my cheekbones, my lashes, my eyes—painted with the cool, expressionless beauty of someone trained to perform. They are almost human. Almost alive. But cold. Polished. Hollow.

The music continues, and the marionettes begin to move with synchronicity. Their limbs lift and settle with mechanical fluidity. Their eyes—my eyes—fix on me as they watch and wait.

I inhale and feel something land on my skin.

I hit at it. It feels like I walked into a spider's web, the connection soft, weightless, and creepy. More fall, and I shudder at that silk-like feeling hitting my skin. They curl around my arms, my neck, my spine, threads of light and shadow so fine they barely exist. They do not pull. They do not bind. They wait. There's no force, just expectation, and my body jerks as instinct overrides reason.

They don't tighten once they land. Instead, they seem to move with me as though they've always been here. As though I've always belonged to them. Some glisten like moonlight. Others are darker and feel as if they're braided with memory and guilt. Still, others are as soft as submission but sharp as obedience.

I tug one, and it hums a low, familiar sound, like my own voice whispering a warning: Be good.

One of the marionettes blinks. The motion is extremely slow and deliberate. As if it's humoring me. When it tilts its head and studies me, something twists in my gut. This one is aware. Too aware.

"Don't fight it, Amelia," it whispers, and my blood chills.

The voice is mine, the one I've used for years when justifying every compromise to myself. I've heard it every moment I swallowed myself to stay palatable.

The music distorts, slowing into something mournful. A lullaby masquerading as comfort.

I move to break free, but more strings bloom from the shadow and wrap around my ankles, my waist, and my spine. Still, they don't command my movements. They invite me to be part of the collective.

A different marionette glides with eerie grace, extending its hand to perfectly mirror my own. The gesture is soft, rehearsed, and familiar.

"This is how you survive," it whispers.

The words settle into my bones like a remembered curse.

Above me, the collective stills. Their strings tighten. They wait for the ritual to begin—the one I performed every day to earn approval. The ritual of poise, perfection, silence. They will not proceed until I take my place.

My knees lock. My whole chest jerks in a broken rhythm. The strings pulse like a hand pressing at the small of my back.

Though I haven't stepped forward, I am onstage.

My fingers tremble. My heels dig into the floor. The marionette lifts its hand again. Beckoning.

"This is how you survive."

Then, every one of them blinks in unison. They open their mouths and speak like a well-rehearsed choir.

"Be a good girl." "Don't you cry." "No one likes a baby."

Their voices layer like a chant, not screamed, but recited in even cadence as they issue more directives.

"Sit up straight." "Do better." "Try harder."

I can barely stand the sound of my voice. The conditioning rubs me raw as it echoes deep inside of me. There is a space still there, born of approval withheld and perfection demanded.

I flinch as one single tear slips loose. The strings respond. Tightening.

The marionettes in the rafters begin to sing in the round.

"Be perfect." "Don't cry." "No one likes a baby…"

It's grotesque. The harmony curdles and decays my resolve as the song taunts and mocks me. The sound creeps over my skin as all the marionettes descend, their joints creaking and their movements jarring. They are neither alive nor dead but something in between.

One comes near. Its painted smile stretches.

"This is how you survive," it says again, softly.

It's at that moment I know what I've been running from, and I know what I've become.

I performed just like these puppets. I wasn't loved but groomed—polished until I mistook control for approval and obedience for affection. I called it love, but it was survival dressed in perfection.

The strings tighten as the marionettes surround me.

My knees give way as I curl in on myself, arms wrapped tightly around me, my head tucking down until my chin hits my chest. It's a posture of surrender I haven't made in years but comes too easily because it's too well remembered.

"A-meeeeeel-ia."

The sound of my name sings through the dark, each syllable dragged like a fingernail along my spine. The last warmth in my chest collapses until it becomes ice. A chill rushes through me, black and complete. I want to disappear inside it, to be swallowed whole.

But I lift my head. With my arms still wrapped around myself, I search the rafters.

There, at the highest perch.

The puppet master.

28

The marionette's limbs flex with a creaking elegance. They're unnervingly fluid, like something that was once human, then forgot how to be.

One by one, their mouths curve, their smiles stretching in perfect, unnatural synchrony. Just a hint at first, a slight lift at the corners, as if they're all sharing the same quiet secret.

My pulse quickens as their limbs jolt, then align, standing with uncanny precision, each movement executed in seamless harmony. Their movements are rigid and mechanical. Their backs straighten, and smiles widen, then go wider still until their lips part to reveal rows of perfectly carved, white, wooden teeth. The pristine gleam of them is sickening. It's too flawless to belong to anything real. Each set of eyes are fixed on me. Unblinking. Frozen. Watching.

A chill crawls up my spine as they move and their stiff limbs clack together. One by one, they assemble in perfect formation, their movements deliberate. The sound of wooden feet ticking across the floor is like a countdown to something inevitable. The theater seems to contract around me, and the air fills with the scent of varnish and dust. My replicas advance around me in perfect rhythm, their presence pressing in on me from all sides like a noose slowly tightening.

I take a step back and stumble to the ground. My breath comes too fast. My chest tightens. A scream catches in my throat. I want to run back to my room, but there's no exit. I'm alone with these creatures. Their eyes never leave me. Their smiles remain wide and unnatural, as if they are savoring this moment as they move as a single entity.

"A-meeeel-iaaa..."

The voice slithers through the air once again, dark and taunting. Nausea hits me in waves. I force myself to look up, to face the woman who shaped me. The one who taught me to always be on the defensive yet stay in control. To never let anyone see weakness and bury kindness in discipline. I contorted compassion into perfection because I knew no other way. After all, she used to tell me, no one is kind to you without wanting something in return. She's the one who bent and broke me. She polished me into a version of myself that my employees cannot stand. One that even I struggle to be around.

She stands behind the marionettes, content to command the army of girls with obedient, painted smiles.

The sight of her guts me. She stands proud, polished, in her finest clothes. Her expression is serene, cold, and calculating. The marionettes freeze when she comes into view. They watch her with reverence and obedience and perfect smiles that never falter.

Our eyes lock.

She *is* the puppet master.

I am no one's puppet!

A surge of rage tears through me. I push myself up from the ground, every muscle burning as something inside me cracks open. The fire in my chest is greater than the pain as fury unleashes.

"No!"

Though I shake, my voice roars through the theater like a war cry. My hands ball into fists. My body trembles—but I've never felt more powerful.

The word hangs in the air, heavy and final, and the marionettes stare, mouths closed and eyes wide.

I spin, my body wild with rage, slashing the air like I'm slicing through centuries of silence. I cut, one by one, the strings which were meant to control me. They unravel and fall, shimmering threads of expectation and fear torn apart by the force of my defiance. The marionettes drop like exhaled lies, splintering into pieces that no longer hold power.

The auditorium air fills with the sharp, final sound of control breaking, and the army of wooden perfection collapses into dust.

When all my ties are severed, my breath comes in ragged gasps. My chest heaves as I stand at the center of the wreckage, surrounded by broken pieces of myself.

Then it hits me. Everything. The rage. The release. The truth.

I don't have to be the way anyone made me. For years, I've been conditioned to perform, obey, and achieve. To be perfect. I've been punished for speaking out. Threatened when I questioned. Reshaped until there was nothing left of me but what I became. A version of myself that was easier to manage than to love.

I became her.

Silence settles as soft as ash. The air stills, and the weight lifts. The sound, the stage, the strings—they disappear. The marionettes vanish, crumbling not into splintered wood but into light. As if they were never real. As if they were only echoes of a past I no longer need.

My stiff desire to control everything is gone—not with a scream or a shatter. It simply fades, like smoke exhaled from an extinguished fire.

As I stand in the middle of it, the auditorium folds in on itself like an origami memory, and tension releases its hold. Quiet ease settles into my ribs and I no longer feel the need for permission to shape my life.

The floor beneath me returns to moss, soft and sacred, pulsing faintly with something alive. The air smells like rain on stone, layered with honeysuckle and the sweet silence that comes with a gentle shower. I rise slowly and look up, relishing each drop of the cleansing. My arms hang heavy at my sides. My knees tremble, not from fear, but from release. Every muscle in my body feels wrung out—but clean. The silence I used to try to fill is no longer hollow. It is peaceful and whole... just like me.

All at once, the weight of everything I've shed catches up to me, and without warning, I sink. I feel emptied of everything that was never mine to carry.

When I investigate the void that, moments ago, was a nightmare, I see it. A wall of light shimmers ahead.

It falls like a curtain from the sky, as if spun from old magic and starlight, and woven with mist and molten gold. It doesn't beckon. It doesn't command. It simply is. Light bends, refracts, and for a moment, it feels like the world inhales.

Then, from the soft shimmer ahead, a figure emerges—not through force or grandeur, but with the calm gravity of something eternal made gentle.

He wears no crown. No thunder accompanies his appearance. And yet, he feels older than time itself. Like a myth. Mercy made into form.

For a long moment, we simply share the same air, letting the silence stretch between us as a bridge. He watches me with eyes that seem made of storm and sorrow, and the quiet, raw hope that follows. When ours meet, it is with reverence, and the quiet between us honors all that has just been undone.

"Who are you?" I ask.

"I am Elias." When he speaks, his voice carries the gravity of one who has never spoken an untruth. "I am called many things. Architect. Elder. Guardian. I am the Watcher."

"And you have watched me?"

"I have," he answers. "I have watched you endure. I have watched you forget. Now, I have watched you remember."

Beneath his voice, another presence flickers, and I feel it. Soft, feminine, and eternal, as she quietly watches me through eyes that have always seen. I don't know how I know, but I'm certain it's Juliette. She, too, has borne witness to my transformation and is present in this sacred space.

He lifts his hand, and though they do not pass through the Veil, I feel his fingertip linger on my forehead. I close my eyes as he draws a single, unseen symbol into my skin. A blessing. A claiming.

"You are more than the cost, Amelia. More than the wound. More than the perfect control you once mistook for safety."

Elias's words settle deep inside my ribs, into a hollow place that no longer feels like an absence.

I don't respond. I don't thank him. Somehow, I feel he doesn't expect me to, but I don't know how I know. It's simply impressed on my heart.

Though my throat still feels raw and my hands still tremble, inside, something shifts. Not because Elias spoke to me. Not because The Hotel put me through this torture. But because I've finally laid down all that I was never meant to hold—and for the first time in my life, I feel free.

All my life, I polished myself into something she could love. And in doing so, I abandoned the one who needed love the most.

My fingers drift toward the key without thinking, and when I look down, the shank is blank—clean, reflective, waiting. The sight makes something inside me tighten, though I can't say why. Elias watches me notice it, his attention sharpening in that quiet, unsettling way of his.

"Who are you, Amelia?" he asks.

The question seems simple. Too simple. I clear my throat. "I'm me, Amelia Daniels."

He holds my gaze, and for a moment it feels as though he's looking past the surface of me—past the name, past the armor, past every polished answer I've ever practiced.

"That is your name," he says softly. "Who are *you*?"

A flicker of frustration rises in me. "I don't know what answer you want from me," I say. "I'm the same person I was when I arrived."

Elias doesn't respond aloud. Instead, something shifts in the space between us; a silent communication that isn't sound and isn't thought, but somehow both. His gaze deepens, and the question unfurls inside my mind as clearly as if he'd spoken it.

You were Control when you arrived. Who are you now, Amelia?

The words land hard. Not cruelly. Truth rarely needs cruelty.

I let the silence hold me while I search for something I've never said before. Something I didn't know waited inside me. Finally, the answer rises.

"I am Serenity," I whisper.

The key warms faintly in my palm, and the word appears.

Behind the Veil
When a soul is seen, the world must shift

THE HOTEL LISTENS.

Amelia stood in the ruin of her own making and did not look away. Not from the strings. Not from the mirrored truths. Not even from the mother figure who shaped her silence into a means of survival. I did not interfere.

Elias watched as the marionettes dissolved and the inner child Amelia carried folded into the marrow of who she is now. That child—once folded behind curated smiles and the discipline of restraint—is hidden no longer. She did not claw her way forward. She was not dragged into the light. She was seen. And in being seen, she returned. Not with noise, but with knowing. For it is not force that reclaims us—it is witnessing. The kind that does not fix, but frees.

The Hotel goes still.

But not from dread.

From awe.

Something sacred settles into its bones—not a hush of hesitation, but reverence. The very walls feel it. They no longer brace against Amelia's resistance. They register the change. They listen. Where once the structure prodded, now it pivots. It is no longer testing her. It is attending to her, listening. . Where once a building prodded, now it adjusts. It has watched her come undone—not in chaos, but in a state of grace—and it has accepted her.

Juliette comes to stand beside Elias. She, too, felt the shift. She does not speak, but her presence wraps the chamber like silk soaked in memory. Her silence was not absence; it was trust. She knew Amelia would not break. She knew the child within would rise and claim her victory. She has always known.

When Elias stepped forward, it was not to claim but to affirm that he did not grant freedom; he simply acknowledged it. The symbol he traced on Amelia's brow was not a mark of passage. It was a seal of remembrance. For what she once tried to forget, she must now remember. She never reached her best self through perfection and control—it was in returning to herself. Her breath is no longer braced. Her posture is no longer stiff. She is not entirely confident and whole, but she is becoming it.

The threads that once held her now trail behind her, severed not by violence but by truth. The truth is this: she was never broken. She was bound. Now, she is not.

Lysander and Vesper stood not as opposites of morality but as opposites of choice. One offered Amelia awakening and brilliance. The other offered her silence sharpened into survival, shaped into dominance. Both were present. Both watched. One held up a mirror. One held a looking glass. But it was Amelia who chose who to become—and who she would no longer be.

The Hotel adjusts, just as Amelia has. They are tethered to one another and respond in kind. As Amelia breaks free, its chambers soften. Its rhythm no longer asks what she must prove. It waited to see what she would choose. It mourned when she remembered the cost. She has raged and reclaimed for the child. Now she is free to become the woman she was never permitted to be.

Beyond the shimmer of the Veil, two forces stir—neither bound by time nor tethered to form. They do not step forward, but their echoes do.

Lysander, Keeper of Origins presses no hand, speaks no word—but a pulse of light fractures outward, like starlight remembering its source. It does not guide. It affirms. The choice she made—to return to herself, not as a performer but as sovereign—sings across the ether, and he receives it as a note added to the eternal chord of becoming. In his realm of sparks and spirals, something shifts. Not loudly. But enough.

Vesper, Dagger of Doubt, lingers in shadow. No movement, no flare—only the sensation of something once poised to strike, now pulling back. Not in defeat, but in study. Rage is not her nature when truth is chosen; she observes it. Commits it to memory. Tucks it into the hollows where hesitation once bloomed. Doubt does not disappear; it is never vanquished. Yet, for this moment, the force behind it goes quiet.

For one luminous instant, all three forces—Amelia, Lysander, and Vesper—exist in balance.

In truth.

Juliette Armand,
Countess de Lumière

The 22nd Day
The Phase of Integration
The Time of the Threaded Moon

I have reached the center of myself, though the Seven Paths of The Labyrinth tried to unmake me. I did not travel the trails there through ease but through a shedding, layer by careful layer, until only truth remained. I have released that which was never mine to carry, and I no longer recoil from the fractures. I now touch them with reverence in much the way a cartographer would trace the outline of a world once feared, then understood. I think more highly of myself now than when I was chattel, used to secure the line and legacy of my family. I now liken my breaks to the gold in cracked porcelain. I refuse to think of them as wounds, but as revelation.

They are not the memory of my breaking, but evidence of my becoming.

I do not yet know where the path bends next for there are no maps here. No lantern held out by another hand to assist me. I do not need it for I no longer seek direction. I will take each Phase as it comes and welcome the challenge of making my own decisions, and I will do these things as a woman shaped by those who feared my softness, and who manipulated me to serve selfish purposes. I am not, and will not be, the reflection of my heritage, polished for the approval of others. I will be—no, I AM the woman I was always meant to be, and I sing in the night beneath all the moons and plants that bloom within their phases.

The Haven is my solace. Its walls do not press in to constrict me; they expand. The stillness here is not silence but promise, and it shifts around me now as gently as a waking memory. Once I feared it was only a chamber of tests, but now it is a sanctuary.

Though I tried, I realize that I am not perfect, but then I was never meant to be.

I am whole. At last, it is more than enough.

In wholeness,
~J

29

Juliette's journal.

It was open and already forming with a message the moment I returned to my room. Though exhausted once again, and barely remembering the walk back, I will always remember the connection I felt to her when I read her words.

We both survived The Labyrinth—and I have a new word on my key.

SERENITY.

Once I exited the Labyrinth, Ethan was waiting for me. He escorted me to my room.

We did not speak. Words were unnecessary, but his presence was comforting.

I arrived back at my room strangely numb, completely untethered from the person I was when I first arrived at The Hotel. As I left the Labyrinth, I felt I was gliding through the hallways like a shadow unhooked from its source, moving without hesitation or thought, but once inside my room, all seemed unchanged.

Except the air.

That had shifted.

The Hotel still watches me with unseen eyes. Where it once pressed in on me with every shift of air, now I feel its presence because it rests inside me.

If The Haven truly shifts for its Chosen, as Esme implied, then The Hotel is a place of my making. It twisted itself around my resistance, wound itself through my silence, and mirrored my undoing in every corner of its magnificent architecture. It is my witness, my provocateur, and now. my reflection. I feel this, though I can't explain how. What stands out most is how I began to sense its cadence shifting with each step I took in the Labyrinth. Somehow it integrated with me and once I realized that my pulse steadied to its beat, I felt the walls of this place soften around me.

Left alone with so many thoughts I could barely compartmentalize them, I rested. I needed it. Food arrived. Then sleep.

True to my insomniatic nature, sleep and I kept our usual distance, and dreams swam behind my eyes. They were all fragmented and disjointed, and felt threatening. Faces surfaced:

My mother and her signature look of disapproval.

The tremble in my throat the first time I failed.

When she taught me how costly imperfection could be in her care.

I also heard my own laughter in that dream. Before it had boundaries.

My dreams and memories didn't show up to haunt me. They were visitors asking to be seen. I didn't fight them.

I couldn't.

The Hotel's truth was too large for old containers. Now, the truth is expanding. It fills the spaces where perfection once lived.

Why did it never occur to me that control wasn't my nature, but my armor?

A note from Esme is waiting for me when I get out of the shower. After drying my hair and getting dressed, she meets me at my door. As we walk side by side, it's as though the walls are washed in gold. The courtyard yawns open. Stretching before us is the path.

"Do you remember the Path of Keys?" she asks.

I nod.

It's brighter now and holds beauty like nothing I've seen. Beneath my feet, glass shimmers in the light. The mosaic seems smooth and ancient and gleams in the hush of the sun's golden rays. But it's the keys that mean the most, and the words that mark them, which make up the stunning arrangement.

Woven through the path, embedded in its very bones, lie hundreds—if not thousands—of keys. Gold. Silver. Bronze. Rose-gold. The winding path is a soothing stream of metal and memory, and leads toward a central pedestal wrapped in purple clematis and bathed in the morning glow.

"This is the Path of Echoes," she says softly as if the stones are listening. "It marks the journey of everyone who dares walk their Haven. Each foot leaves a trace. Each soul has a resonance that lingers. Every choice you've made, Amelia... they still move through the world like waves that have yet to break."

Her words fall gently like petals on still water, and beneath my feet, the keys begin to hum as if they recognize my presence. I feel it in the hollows of my heart where empathy was once absent. Each key we've passed whispers—not in words, but in sensation. I think of the weight of those who've journeyed before me. They aren't ghosts but echoes now, and their transformation has not faded. Once, I thought the path was lonely. Now, I feel part of a collective I know is sacred.

Esme turns toward me, holding something in her hands.

"What's this?"

She takes my hand and places a velvet pouch into it. When I loosen the drawstring and reach inside. My fingers brush something cool and smooth. It hums with a purpose similar to the key I surrendered. As I lift it out, a fine gold chain spills out and puddles into my palm. At its center is a dark stone, round and banded in gold. There is a tiny gold key attached to its center.

Esme takes it, circles around me, and fastens the clasp, her touch feather-light.

"Onyx is born of shadow. Its vibrations steady the heart, protects what is still tender, and absorbs the energy that you are no longer meant to carry. Let it keep you grounded as you rise." She pauses. "It's just a reminder, Amelia," she adds. "Don't ever fear opening the parts of you that are hidden. Every door within leads to somewhere worth discovering."

Her words feel like a blessing as the key settles in the hollow at the base of my throat.

"Your journey here is not the end." Her voice floats in the morning light. "It is the door. You have so much more life to live. Enjoy it."

Instantly, her words take root.

I close my hand around the necklace, and Esme departs. I move to return to my room, but before I go, I glance once more at the Path of Echoes.

The sun catches the mosaic, and something glints back—my key, gleaming among the others. I smile, not because I am finished, but because I've finally begun.

Down in the lobby, I prepare to leave The Hotel. I no longer feel the heaviness I arrived with. There's a quieter weight replacing it.

Beyond the iron gates, the car waits. Its polished black frame catches the fragile blush of dawn, the last remnants of a restful night brushing silver along its curves. The road ahead shimmers, blacktop laced with crushed glass that scatters morning light like fallen stars. It feels more like a threshold. A crossing filled with new choices.

Ethan stands at the gate, steady as ever. His linen shirt shifts slightly with the breeze. His gaze finds mine with the kind of knowing that asks for nothing and understands everything.

I walk toward him, the key at my throat warming in the sunlight. Each step feels etched into memory like The Hotel is recording my exit with reverence. When I reach him, I pause. What rises in my chest is not sadness; it's anticipation for new beginnings.

"Ethan. Thank you. For everything." The words are small. Insufficient. But they are what I have. "Your presence made all the difference."

He smiles, faint but certain. "It was a privilege to be your guide." His tone is calm and deep, like still water holding the secrets of the sea.

Gratitude presses sharp and aching against my ribs. I lean forward and kiss his cheek, letting it linger—not as a farewell to him but as a parting of the woman I was when I first arrived.

"Goodbye, Ethan."

His gaze does not waver. "Goodbye, Amelia." He holds the moment, then gently and softly speaks. "Remember, the key is always with you."

I nod. The gesture carries what words cannot. The driver grabs the handle of my suitcase and loads it in the car as I let the morning settle into me, and make a memory of the jasmine and dew. I turn toward the car. The door stands open, waiting without urgency. My driver is quiet. This departure is one of many, I'm sure, that he has witnessed.

Inside, the door closes with a soft, sealing hush, and we begin to move. Stillness spreads through me as my fingers find the key around my throat. It doesn't feel like a souvenir, but more like a vow I've made to myself...

To live my truth.

Before the road curves and the shimmer of The Hotel flares one final time, something stirs. A pull. A gentle flicker beneath the surface, insistent like the chilly sensation of someone watching me from the dark.

The pull tightens, and I look back. I feel The Architects and Shrouds. Their presence does not vanish with the light. Through the rear window, The Hotel stands bathed in gold, silent and draped in ivy, unmoving.

Then—slowly—it begins to dissolve. The edges blur, the windows soften, and the walls surrender their shape. It melts into the morning like watercolor sinking into paper. A ribbon of mist curls around it, patient and alive. The deep purple ivy, glass, wood, and iron are disappearing into mist.

It's gone—but a message is pressing into my bones just as the words pressed into my key.

I hold the key to my future. I always did.

31

Stillness settles over the boardroom as I step inside, the kind that pricks the skin and coils low in the belly, demanding not noise but reckoning. The air is thick with unspoken expectations, tension wound tight beneath polished words and practiced neutrality. I feel the eyes of my employees tracking my every movement, calculating, bracing, and waiting for the hammer to fall. They expect retaliation and cold, measured dominance. That would be reasonable if I were a woman returning to reclaim her throne through force of will.

But I'm not the woman they remember.

I'd already met with the Board earlier this morning. There were no fireworks, no demands, no need for raised voices. Just a conversation. I told them I understood their concerns—that I saw now what I hadn't before. They weren't trying to undermine me. They were trying to protect something I built, something I love. I assured them that the version of me standing here now was not a figure of control, but one of clarity. They didn't argue.

Now, I cross the room, each step deliberate. My heels click softly against the floor, a sound that once announced power now simply marks presence. I move to the head of the conference table, but I don't sit. The room is full, and I let the silence stretch, taut and deliberate, until it hums against their nerves and presses into their anticipation. The longer I wait, the more unsure they become. It's the first sign that the balance has already shifted.

I scan their faces—guilt, defiance, unease. Once, I would have mirrored that unease with tighter control, wielding perfection like a weapon. But The Hotel stripped me of that illusion. What remains isn't hollow. It's honest.

I draw in a breath and rest both hands on the table.

"When I last stood in this room, I was leading from fear—of failure, of chaos, of not being enough. That fear made me difficult to work with. And though no one said it aloud, I could feel it. I understand why some of you took your concerns to the Board. And while I wish it had been done differently, I'm not here to retaliate."

The room is quiet but not still. Shifts in posture ripple through the space. Surprise. Curiosity.

"I've spent some time away. Reflecting. Confronting who I'd become and why. What I've come to realize is this: I was holding on too tightly, trying to control every detail, every outcome. And in doing so, I stopped trusting. I lost sight of what actually matters—people. This team. You."

The words don't shake me. They steady me.

"I've made the choice to forgive. And I hope you'll forgive me, too." My voice doesn't falter. "We can't undo the past. But we can decide what we do next. I'm here because I still believe in this company. In what we've built—together. And I'm willing to lead differently. But that only works if we're all in."

One of the senior executives leans forward, clearing his throat.

"What do you propose, Ms. Daniels?"

I meet his eyes without flinching. "We start by resetting expectations. No more silence when something isn't working. No more perfectionism posing as leadership. I want transparency. I want collaboration. I want accountability—from all of us, including me."

I let that settle. I don't push.

"If anyone feels they can't be part of that, I'll understand. But if you stay, we move forward together. Not perfectly. But with purpose."

A long pause follows. Then—movement. Shoulders soften. A few nods. It won't all be healed in a day, but something has shifted. The room exhales.

The meeting disperses with quiet murmurs. No power plays. No cold goodbyes. Just people—maybe even teammates again.

Back in my office, I stand in the silence, which now feels warm, not brittle. I brush my fingers across the leather cover of my day planner. Then I reach for the phone and buzz Sophie.

"Hey," I say. "Do you want to grab lunch?"

There's a beat. "Who? You and me?"

I laugh softly. "Yes. You and me."

"Absolutely," she says, no hesitation this time. "I'll meet you in the lobby."

I sling my purse over my shoulder and step out, but just as I cross the threshold of my office, I bump into someone rounding the corner.

"I'm so sorry," I say, startled. The scent that hits me is warm and familiar—soap, cedar, and something else that doesn't belong here. Something that once was mine.

I look up.

"Christian?"

He blinks. "Amelia?"

We both pause. And then—

"What are you doing—" we say in unison, then laugh.

"You first," he says, voice as deep as ever.

"This is my company."

He smiles. "I was just meeting my cousin. He works in your legal department."

"Small world," I murmur.

We linger for a moment, suspended in a moment that hums with memory. Then Sophie calls my name from down the hall, and the moment breaks—but not completely.

Because sometimes, the past doesn't knock. It brushes your arm in a hallway and reminds you that some doors don't stay closed forever, and some stories are never really finished.

Behind the Veil
Somewhere within the threads of time

Far beyond the walls of The Hotel, past the sea mist and the spiral staircase no map could contain, The Haven stands as it always has, rooted outside of time, alive in the folds of becoming.

In the chamber where no one speaks, unless the silence asks for it, Elias watches.

A ripple has begun. Not with thunder. Not with spectacle. But with the quiet return of a woman to her own becoming. A fracture once hidden now gleams with gold. A voice once swallowed now hums with the gravity of truth.

To Elias's right, Lysander stands in a hush so deep it seems to stretch across centuries, his gaze reflecting the shimmer of futures not yet named. To his left, Vesper drapes herself in shadow, fingers woven together not in stillness, but in restraint. Her silence is not absence—it's anticipation threaded with ache, the kind that remembers what it costs to forget.

She watches the space where another must make a choice while the pain of the past still echoes, and the faint tremor of hope and warning crosses her features like the passing of a cloud.

"It will not be as easy for the next one," Vesper says quietly. "The world teaches them to forget."

Elias's voice is steady, rooted deeper than time. "This one would rather forget. She carries the burden of her birth. She has not yet chosen to become what she was meant to be."

Lysander steps forward, his voice low and reverent. "How will The Haven find her?"

Elias turns his gaze toward the unseen Wheel of Time, his voice a soft certainty. "The Haven listens for the souls who fracture silently. It watches for the ones who ache without knowing why. It will find the next Chosen and present itself accordingly. I feel it already stirs."

Silence folds itself into the room, not emptiness, but expectancy. A living hush. One by one, they vanish. The chamber empties.

Only Juliette remains.

She has been present all along, cloaked in a quiet so deep she has become part of the stones. When the chamber empties and returns to stillness, she rises. Her bare feet whisper against the ancient floor. The lamps flicker with a windless flame as she passes, and the air seems to bow in her wake. She watches. She remembers.

She anticipates the arrival of the next Chosen.

The End

Then read on for more about the mythical world of *The Haven.*

The Architects
Of Eternity

"Before the first stone was laid, before the first question was asked, they waited."

The Architects of Eternity are not ethereal overseers or passive guides. They are those who have been since the beginning of time. The ones who awaken life into the spaces they shape. Their presence is embedded in the walls and the air. Their unseen energy makes seekers feel as though they have stepped into something meant for them alone. There is a separation between the physical and the metaphysical, but every brick laid, every light shifted, and every ritual created is meant to be felt at the deepest level.

They are the unseen hands, the quiet guides, and the weavers of destiny. Through the spaces they shape and the mysteries they guard, they create sanctuaries where transformation unfolds. Where seekers find answers and the courage to ask the right questions. Eternity is not a place but a journey they build, one revelation at a time.

They are not whispered myths or celestial overseers. They are felt in the hush before the realization dawns, in the pulse of light that flickers when the truth is on the verge of breaking through. The Architects of Eternity do not command, nor do they interfere. Instead, they construct, patiently, purposefully, both in form and in the unseen threads that bind a seeker to the journey they were always meant to take.

Their presence is not loud, yet it lingers in the quiet stillness between decision and surrender, in the weight of a door that swings open at precisely the right moment, in the way air thickens with something unspeakable before revelation strikes. They are the unseen force that fills the lungs of transformation and the bones of the sanctuaries that stand as both refuge and reckoning.

Each Architect carries a singular purpose: to sew light into the frayed seams of a soul, not with force, but with patience until the spirit remembers it was always whole.

Elias: The Eternal Guide. He is the bridge, the constant. The Watcher. The presence who does not demand to be seen but is always felt. If The Haven is the soul, the venues it creates are its whispered invitation. Elias is the hand that guides without ever touching. The voice that does not echo yet is always heard. He does not speak often, for his wisdom is not given; it is uncovered, as if it had always belonged to the Chosen, waiting to be remembered. The weight of his presence is timeless, but his movements are light and deliberate, as if shaped by the very essence of patience. When he is near, the air steadies, carrying the unshakable knowing that whatever is coming has already been set in motion. Elias is not the architect of fate nor the master of free will. He is the one who ensures both find their course.

Lysander: The Keeper of Origins. He is the first memory, the forgotten thread that binds what was to what must be. Lysander's work is not seen in the physical walls of The Haven or The Hotel; it is felt in the silent truths that rise unbidden when a seeker stands too long in front of a mirror or lingers too long at a crossroads. He does not shape structure or light; he tends to the original flame, the part of each soul that existed before fear, before forgetting. His presence is the ache that pulls at the heart when old dreams resurface. It is the gravity in the air that reminds a soul they were born whole before the world asked them to fragment. Lysander is not a guide nor a judge. He is the quiet witness to beginnings, the guardian of everything a seeker once knew but learned to abandon. To stand in the spaces he touches is to remember. To walk through the corridors of The Hotel is to brush against the ancient question he asks without words: "Who were you before the world demanded you become someone else?" His gift is not to answer but to awaken the knowing that has always been waiting inside.

Kaelah: The Sculptor of Thresholds. Her graceful hands do not merely carve; they breathe life into wood and stone. Her gift embeds whispers into the grains and etches truth through the veins drifting through marble slates. Her doors do not separate spaces; they usher seekers into the depths of themselves. Each carving is not simply decoration; it is a beckoning, an unspoken question, a promise that whatever lies beyond is precisely what is needed. To pass through one of her creations is to be acknowledged, recognized by something ancient and unseen, as though the very walls of the sanctuary know why the seeker has arrived.

Cassian: The Builder Between Worlds. There is no dust on his hands, though they have shaped the foundation of a place existing beyond time. The walls of The Hotel do not simply stand; they remember. Cassian does not construct with stone alone. He builds with memory, purpose, and the aching need of the unseen. His corridors are not places to pass through, but thresholds that remember. Every beam hums with intention, every arch curves with unspoken invitation. The walls he shapes do not merely stand; they listen. They wait. They hold space for the words a seeker cannot yet say. In the silence between steps, his craftsmanship becomes presence—meeting the soul not with answers, but with the reverence of being known.

Selene: The Keeper of Stories and Dreams. She does not write in ink or bind her stories on pages. Selene's tales are written in the very fabric of space, in the shifting of walls, in the echoes of dreams that take shape the moment a seeker enters. Her work is delicate and overwhelming, a subtle force that ensures every corner of The Haven and The Hotel is crafted not by accident but by necessity. She does not decide what is revealed. She simply ensures it will be. In the hush of a forgotten corridor, in the curve of a staircase that leads only where one is truly ready to go, Selene's touch lingers, unseen but undeniable.

Theron: The Master of Light and Atmosphere. There is no structure without breath, no space that does not pulse with the energy of those who inhabit it. Theron does not build walls; he creates the space between them, the shift in the air that dictates whether one feels safe enough to exhale or unsettled enough to question. The light bends at his will, and shadows stretch or retreat by his design. A corridor may feel endless or comforting, and a chamber may whisper of revelation or surrender. His gift is not in what is seen but in what is felt the moment one steps inside. He sculpts not the physical but the atmosphere, ensuring that even the air inside The Hotel and The Haven becomes its own guide.

Amara: The Weaver of Elements. Her presence is the scent before memory strikes, the warmth in the air that speaks of comfort or longing. She does not command the senses; she beckons them to awaken.

Through the texture of fabric against fingertips, the sound of distant chimes carried on a nonexistent breeze, and the way light filters through a room at precisely the right angle, Amara's touch is felt in the most minor details that make a place feel like destiny. She ensures that transformation is not only a mental process but a full-bodied experience that lingers in the breath, skin, and marrow.

Dorian: The Guardian of Mysteries. Not all paths are straight. Not all answers are obvious. Some truths require wandering. Dorian does not craft mere corridors or rooms; he builds questions into the very structure of The Hotel. He ensures that doors do not always open the first time and that staircases lead somewhere different if approached from another angle. His work is for the seekers who do not yet know what they seek and need to be nudged toward their own curiosity, discomfort, and wonder. His designs are not meant to confuse but to awaken the long-silenced instinct to explore.

Naia: The Oracle and Timekeeper. Time is not a straight line within The Hotel. It does not pass; it exists. Naia ensures that each seeker arrives precisely when they are meant to and that synchronicity is not an accident but a carefully woven thread. She is the whisper of déjà vu, the subtle alignment of moments that feel too perfect to be merely coincidence. Naia's presence is not overwhelming; it is slight. She is the gentle nudging felt in every shift of unseen forces that guide a person to The Hotel's doorstep. For Naia, the past, present, and future are not separate; they are woven into the very walls, waiting for those who are ready to step into them.

Aeris: The Song of Creation. She was not born of time but of longing. When Lysander created Aeris, he asked each of the Architects to give one pure gift, one strand of beauty, wonder, or kindness, to weave into her spirit. All but Elias did. She was shaped of everything bright and uncorrupted, a living melody of what was good before the world fractured. Yet her very existence made her dangerous to the Shrouds of Oblivion. They could not destroy her, but they hid her behind the fourth veil, where she slumbers, unaware of the full power she carries. Aeris is neither a guide nor a builder but potential itself — the seed of new beginnings. Those who dream of a better world dream her into being, though they do not know her name.

The Architects of Eternity are the breath of transformation and the bones of the sanctuaries that hold it.

THE SHROUDS OF OBLIVION

"Before trust knew betrayal, before truth learned to lie, and before wounds had names, they whispered. Not to be heard but to silence."

The Shrouds of Oblivion are the silent mirror to the Architects of Eternity. Where the Architects weave light into hidden places, knitting strength, and hope and becoming into the soul, the Shrouds move in silence, seeking not to destroy but to unravel. They slip between the seams of certainty, loosening threads one quiet beat at a time until wholeness falters and purpose dims. Their presence is not an assault; it is an erosion. Quiet, relentless, inevitable. Where the Architects build sanctuaries of remembrance, the Shrouds invite forgetting. Where the Architects sculpt new beginnings, the Shrouds birth doubt, despair, and apathy. Their work is not loud, yet it lingers, like smoke after flame, like a song you can no longer hear but cannot forget. They do not command ruin. They allow it to bloom.

Each Shroud carries a singular purpose: not to topple the soul in one great collapse but to unravel it thread by thread until nothing remains but a shadow.

Kael: The Harbinger of Chaos. Kael stands as the leader and most powerful of The Shrouds of Oblivion, embodying the raw, untamed force of destruction. His presence does not simply disrupt. It consumes. Reality bends and splinters around him, dismantling stability and unraveling hope. Kael does not move with rage or haste; he moves with certainty, knowing that once chaos begins, it is nearly impossible to bind again. He is the origin of collapse, the force that unbuilds worlds.

Malrik: The Tempest of Ruin. Where Kael devours, Malrik dismantles. The Tempest of Ruin brings devastation not through force but through strategy, unmaking foundations long before the storm strikes. He is patient, weaving betrayal into ambition and doubt into loyalty. His strength is inevitability, the slow, grinding destruction no wall can withstand. By the time his work is seen, it is already too late.

Nyx: The Shadow of Despair. Nyx weaves illusions so potent that even truth recoils. Reality itself fractures beneath her presence. She whispers fears into the minds of her victims, twisting their perceptions until despair blooms unchecked. Light fades in her presence, and the strongest minds falter, questioning what is real, what is possible, and whether anything was ever meant to survive.

Vesper: The Dagger of Doubt. Vesper slips between decisions, cutting resolve with surgical precision. She does not need to tear down walls; she needs only a single crack, a single thought of uncertainty. Her gift is hesitation, planted so subtly that even the boldest lose their footing. Where she walks, conviction crumbles and hesitation becomes surrender.

Dain: The Architect of Desolation. Dain does not destroy through violence but through decay. Dreams wither in his presence, ambition crumbles to dust. He does not break hope with a strike; he rots it from within until even the most beautiful aspirations feel empty and obsolete. His power is slow, suffocating, and absolute.

Solrik: The Whisper of Betrayal. Solrik does not speak in commands; he slips doubt into loyalty, and suspicion into brotherhood. He sows division with the gentlest of seeds, allowing alliances to fall apart from the inside. Trust is his battlefield, and he leaves no bond unscarred. Where he lingers, friendships wither into enemies, and solitude becomes inescapable.

Taryn: The Phantom of Regret. Taryn is the warden of the past, a phantom who binds souls with the chains of what could have been. She resurrects every failure, every wrong turn, replaying them until forward motion feels impossible. Her victims do not need prisons; they build their own, locked in endless cycles of guilt and sorrow they can no longer escape.

Varos: The Abyss of Hopelessness. Varos is the void into which ambition falls and never returns. His presence strips victories of meaning and drains future plans of energy. In his shadow, nothing feels worth striving for, and even the act of dreaming becomes an unbearable weight. To encounter Varos is to be swallowed by the certainty that nothing will ever change.

Luthien: The Warden of Fear. Luthien does not chase fear—he carves it. With hands like shadow, his chill is a frost that kisses as it kills, he sculpts nightmares from memory and buries them in the soft places of the mind. His presence is not violent. It is slow, invasive. A flicker at the edge of sight. A whisper too close to the ear. Under his watch, fear does not arrive—it settles, becomes law, seeps beneath the skin until even silence feels like threat. He does not command terror. He lets it bloom.

Eryx: The Collector of Suffering. Eryx feeds on pain, hoarding suffering like a dragon hoards gold. He ensures wounds never heal, laughter turns bitter, and hope becomes another blade to twist. Every small agony is a feast to him. His victims are not merely hurt; they are hollowed out, made monuments to endurance stretched too far.

The Shrouds of Oblivion are not monsters. They are erosion itself. They do not shatter; they unravel. They do not destroy; they unmake. They wait for those who forget that wholeness must be fiercely guarded, moment by moment, wound by wound.

The Shrouds of Oblivion are the shadow beneath every threshold and the unraveling of dreams too fragile to stand. They have only one restriction: they cannot claim a Chosen's life. But they can make them yearn for release.

DD Lorenzo is an award-winning author of Women's Fiction and Romantic Suspense novels. She loves coffee, long lunches with good friends, and fresh flowers to balance her obsession with anti-heroes. You can find her most days plotting and planning her character's lives from her beach house on
the Delaware shore.

To stay updated with DD's books, please visit her website at www.ddlorenzo.com and sign up for her newsletter. Want the inside scoop? Join DD's reader group, DDs Diamonds, at www.facebook.com/groups/ddsdiamonds

Stay connected with DD

Website:
www.ddlorenzo.net

facebook.com/ddlorenzo.author
x.com/ddlorenzobooks
instagram.com/ddlorenzobooks
pinterest.com/ddlorenzo
bookbub.com/authors/d-d-lorenzo
amazon.com/DD-Lorenzo/e/B00GA5ARJ8
goodreads.com/D_D_Lorenzo

Other Titles by DD Lorenzo

The IMPERFECTION Series

No Perfect Beginning: An IMPERFECTION Series Prequel

No Perfect Man

No Perfect Time

No Perfect Couple

No Perfect Secret

No Perfect Woman

The ROCK HILLS Series

Boundless Hearts: A ROCK HILLS Origin Story

Bone Dust: Rock Hills Book 1

Standalones

Indiscretion (An Aleatha Romig's Infidelity World Novella)

Heels, Rhymes, & Nursery Crimes

(A multi-author series)

Twinkle, Twinkle Little Star: Fragile Flower to Femme Fatale

www.ingramcontent.com/pod-product-compliance
Lightning Source LLC
LaVergne TN
LVHW041738060526
838201LV00046B/852